Maverick

The Perished Riders MC - Book 1

Nicola Jane

Copyright © 2021 by Nicola Jane

All rights reserved.

No portion of this book may be reproduced in any form without written permission from the publisher or author, except as permitted by U.K. copyright law.

Meet the team

Cover Designer: Charli Childs, Cosmic Letterz Design
Editor: Rebecca Vazquez
Proofreader: Jackie Ziegler
Formatting: Nicola Miller
Publisher: Nicola Jane

Disclaimer:

This book is a work of fiction. The names, characters, places, and incidents are all products of the author's imagination and are not to be construed as real. Any similarities are entirely coincidental.

Spelling Note:

Please note, this author resides in the United Kingdom and is using British English. Therefore, some words may be viewed as incorrect or spelled incorrectly, however, they are not.

Acknowledgments

For Paul, my best friend, my husband, and the reason I am following this crazy journey. Thank you for supporting me, for championing me at every turn, for being the most amazing, hardworking, and funny person I know. This is all possible because you pushed me to take the leap. I love you and will always be forever grateful to have such an amazing man in my life. I am truly lucky.

To Fay and Emma. Thank you for sharing some of the most horrific stories I've ever heard and allowing me to use them as part of this story. I'm sorry it put a downer on our ladies' night. I'll choose my moments more carefully next time lol.

It highlights the many people suffering silently from domestic abuse, but you also are both living proof that you can survive, and you girls are two of the strongest, kind, and amazing women I know. Thank you for being in my life and allowing me to be in yours.

My readers, this is my second MC series and I hope you all love this one as much as you do the Kings Reapers. Thanks for following me and sticking with me, and I hope to bring you more in this series soon.

Trigger Warning

The material in this book may be viewed as offensive to some readers, including graphic language, sexual situations, murder, violence, talk of domestic abuse and talk of childhood sexual abuse (however, the author does not go into detail).

You may consider other parts of this story triggering, ones that I maybe don't. Maverick would like to remind you that this is his story and he can speak and act how he likes, as can his ol' lady. If you find their behaviour troubling, you can put your complaint in writing, addressed to the president of the club.

Happy reading xx

Contents

PLAYLIST		IX
1.	PROLOGUE	1
2.	CHAPTER ONE	3
3.	CHAPTER TWO	9
4.	CHAPTER THREE	21
5.	CHAPTER FOUR	29
6.	CHAPTER FIVE	37
7.	CHAPTER SIX	49
8.	CHAPTER SEVEN	59
9.	CHAPTER EIGHT	67
10.	CHAPTER NINE	77
11.	CHAPTER TEN	87
12.	CHAPTER ELEVEN	97
13.	CHAPTER TWELVE	103
14.	CHAPTER THIRTEEN	115
15.	CHAPTER FOURTEEN	124
16.	CHAPTER FIFTEEN	133
17.	CHAPTER SIXTEEN	145

18.	CHAPTER SEVENTEEN	159
19.	CHAPTER EIGHTEEN	169
20.	CHAPTER NINETEEN	183
21.	CHAPTER TWENTY	193
	A note from me to you	201

PLAYLIST

Stitches - Shawn Mendes
Part of Me - Katy Perry
No Love - Eminem ft. Lil Wayne
What The Hell - Avril Lavigne
Stronger (What Doesn't Kill You) - Kelly Clarkson
Take Care - Drake ft. Rihanna
I Hate Everything About You - Three Days Grace
You Save Me - Alicia Keys ft. Snoh Aalegra
My Favorite Part - Mac Miller ft. Ariana Grande
breathin - Ariana Grande
Rescue - Lauren Daigle
Praying - Kesha
You Say - Lauren Daigle
You're Gonna Be OK - Brian & Jenn Johnson
Scars To Your Beautiful - Alessia Cara
Fix You - Coldplay
You Are The Reason - Calum Scott ft. Leona Lewis
I'll Find You - Lecrae ft. Tori Kelly

PROLOGUE

MAVERICK

25 years earlier...

I stare up into the eyes I know so well. They reassure me things will be okay. All I have to do is exactly what he says. In my ten-year-old brain, I can almost pretend this is a game. One like Grim and I play back at the club. My dad, Eagle, President of The Perished Riders MC, hands me the cold metal object. It's heavier than I thought, and I stare hard at the worn handle of the Glock-19. "Now, son, don't let me down on this," he says firmly, and I nod. I'd never let my old man down—he's my hero.

There's a rustling behind us and everyone turns just as my mum, Brea, comes running through the trees. "Wyatt," she yells, and my dad groans.

"Brea, not now," he says, his tone warning. The other guys begin to shift uncomfortably. I don't blame them, because when Mum's Irish temper comes out, she's crazy.

"I told you no," she screams. "Kilian, put that thing down," she commands, pointing at the Glock still clasped in my sweaty hands.

"Brea, go home," snaps Dad. His face is red with anger, and I wonder how Mum never cowers away when he's like this.

"I will not let you do this to my son," she cries. "Kilian, put it down," she repeats. I look at my dad, who shakes his head, so I keep the gun gripped tightly.

"You did this. It started with you and him," Dad spits out. "Copper, take her home," he orders his Enforcer. "Tie her up, if you have to, but don't let her back here."

I watch as Copper steps towards my mum. She backs away, shaking her head angrily. "You lay one finger on me and so help me God, I'll—" She doesn't finish because Copper grabs her and throws her over his shoulder, carrying her away kicking and screaming.

We wait in silence until her screams of hate become quieter. Dad finally turns to me and nods. "When you're ready," he says.

I move my feet slightly apart, just like he's shown me a million times, then I raise the gun and keep my arms straight. Focusing my eyes on my target, I clear my mind and turn off the screams in my head. I can't afford to mess this up because my future depends on this moment right here. This is my time. If I don't do this, I'll never have the respect of the other club members, and without respect, a club president is nothing more than a prospect. I play my dad's words over and over as I take deep breaths in and out. On my third exhale, I release the safety on the gun. My target begins to fidget, a muffled moan escaping. My arms begin to ache and I move my head from side to side, loosening the tense muscles in my neck. I suck in another breath, and on the release, I pull the trigger.

CHAPTER ONE

MAVERICK

Present day...

I've been back in London, at the club, for three months. In that time, I've buried my dad, taken the President patch, reassigned positions within the club, and made a start on revamping The Perished Riders MC clubhouse.

"Take charge," I tell Hadley, my younger sister, as I hand her the delivery note. She heads outside to the van to oversee the delivery of the club's new furniture. I watch my men removing the old furniture from the main room to dump out with the trash. No offence to my old man, but the seventies vintage look went out decades ago and there's no place for flower-patterned couches or glass coffee tables.

"Thank Christ for that," mutters Grim, my VP, as a stained and tattered couch is tossed in the bin. "I swear that couch had bugs, it's that old." I nod in agreement, but it feels bittersweet removing the furniture that Dad once chose. "And just think how many times the guys have fucked a whore over that thing." Grim shudders.

"Where's Meli?" I ask, changing the subject. Hadley's twin is on a lockdown of sorts. She's been off the rails for far too long, and since Grim and I have returned, we've been trying to gain some semblance of control. It was Grim's idea to ground her, even though she's an adult. She doesn't give two fucks about her safety, but now it's my job to take care of her.

"Last time I checked, she was sulking in her room. I thought the promise of new decor might lure her out, but . . ." He shrugs.

My younger twin sisters are like chalk and cheese. Amelia is strong willed and feisty. I let Grim deal with her, because he enjoys pissing her off. Hadley, on the other hand, is quiet and keeps herself in the shadows. She likes to read books and take walks. She hides herself under baggy clothing despite being beautiful. It's almost like she doesn't believe she's worthy to shine. I put that down to our childhood.

Dad was president of The Perished Riders right up until he died a few months ago. He wasn't a loving, kind father. He kept us at arm's length but gave us valuable lessons with his harsh words. Nothing was ever good enough, or enough full stop. When it came to the twins, he treated Meli like a troublesome, annoying animal he had to put up with, while he handled Hadley like a precious stone, too perfect to even look at. If she dared to show a little personality, he'd scowl until she withered back into the shadows.

I was his golden child, the one who he could teach all his sadistic ways. The first time I killed a man was at ten years old. He was my mum's lover and Dad's VP. Killing Viper sticks with me like fucking super glue. It was no wonder I took to the road a few years ago. I couldn't take his control a second longer, so Grim and I fucked our way around the country. But Dad's sudden death put a stop to that, and now, we're back here to sort his mess out.

Crow, the product of Mum's affair, stalks over with a face like thunder. "Are you happy? Getting rid of every last trace of him?" I don't know why he has this loyalty towards the man who ordered his biological father's death. My dad might have raised him, but it wasn't out of love. He forced Mum to keep Viper's kid so she'd be reminded every day of the mistake she'd made.

"Brother, the furniture is older than this damn building. I think he picked up half this shit from charity shops."

"It doesn't matter. It was part of this place."

"Christ, Crow," I sigh, "it's just furniture. I'm having a painting of Eagle's miserable face done right over there," I say, pointing towards the blank wall. "I'm not trying to wipe his memory away, I just wanna tidy this shithole up."

Nelly, our new barmaid, arrives for her shift. She looks distracted, so I make my way over. She's recently left an abusive relationship, and I wanna make sure that shit ain't bothering her. "You okay?"

She nods but looks far from it. "Yeah, just something playing on my mind."

"Anything I can help with?"

She shakes her head before sighing heavily. "It's my new neighbours. I told you before how I was worried about the woman there. I hear them fighting all the time and, I don't know, it just brings back memories. I know if someone had heard my screams, I would have wanted their help. Do you think I should get involved?"

"I dunno, that's a tricky one. They might just have that kind of relationship. She might not want you interfering, but why don't you start by befriending her?"

"Maybe," she muses. "It's just . . . I never see her. I hear them all the time, but I've never once seen her leave the house."

"You could always call the cops when they're arguing." I hate the cops, but Nelly seems like a good-standing citizen, so it's something I should advise her.

"That's the problem. He *is* a cop."

RYLEE

If someone were to stumble across my internet search page, they'd be able to guess my story. It tells so much about a person, doesn't it? For instance, right now, I'm searching 'the best foundation to cover black bruising'. And I'm not the only person to search for it—the words come up before I've finished typing.

"Right, I'm off to work." His voice makes me jump with fright, like I'm doing something wrong. I'm not. I'm covering up what he did wrong but saying that would start a whole new argument. "Why do you look so guilty? What are you doing?" he asks, a smile pulling on his lips. It isn't the kind of smile one gives if they're joking around. He wants an answer.

"Makeup," I say, making sure I keep my tone light and relaxed. That's the key, remaining calm. "I'm looking online for makeup." He holds out his hand and waits patiently as I pass him the mobile. He glances at the screen, rolls his eyes, and stuffs it in his back pocket. He'll take it with him to work, cutting off my contact with the outside world. I've often asked what I'd do in an emergency, and his only reply was 'there'd never be one'. So, I always make sure nothing is left on—the oven, my hair straighteners, any gas appliances—because then there really won't be.

"I said you could use my phone to play a game. It was a reward for your good behaviour just then." He glances at the messed-up sheets on the bed.

"Sorry. I'd really like to take a walk today. It's going to be sunny, and Ella needs fresh air." I know what the answer will be, but I won't ever give up trying.

He scoffs, shrugging into his jacket. "It's a new area, you'll get lost. I'll be home around ten this evening."

"Please, Grant," I mumble. I hate begging, but it seems to be the only way these days.

"It's almost pathetic," he says and groans with irritation. He heads for the front door, and I follow. "Where will you be at ten o'clock?" he asks, a small, cruel smile playing on his lips.

"Right here," I whisper sadly.

"I love you," he says, kissing me hard on the mouth, causing me to wince. My lip's split and bruised, and his kisses are never gentle, even when he knows I'm hurt.

"I love you too," I say. I don't . . . I hate him.

Grant opens the door, and I stand in his shadow. No one is allowed to see me like this, especially not his work colleague, who's waiting patiently in the car outside. She's only been working with him for a month, since we'd moved to London to escape too many questions at his old job. "About time," she shouts playfully, winding the window down. He laughs, waving his hand at her.

"Remember what I said, Rylee," he mutters under his breath, hardly moving his lips at all. "I won't be pleased if you disobey me."

"I won't," I say.

"Is that Rylee?" shouts Lois. "How are you?"

"Good," I say, my voice sounding croaky from my earlier crying. Grant turns to face me, keeping me out of view. She can't see me clearly anyway, our garden is long and she's right out on the road.

"Kiss me like you love me," he demands. Reaching up, I place my hands on his broad shoulders. I tilt my head slightly, and his hands cup my face. Our lips gently brush against each other, and as we pull apart, he kisses my nose. "I hope you're in a much better mood when I return," he says. I nod, pushing away any bitter thoughts I have of sticking my thumbs into his eyeballs until he screams in pain.

"Have a good shift," I say.

He steps out into the bright sunshine, and I make sure to keep in the shadows. As he pulls the door closed, I see the way Lois's head tips to one side, like she's trying to get a better look at my face. I wait for him to lock the door before rushing upstairs to the bedroom window, where I keep far enough back for them not to see me. I mustn't ever look out the windows. It's another rule.

Grant gets into Lois's car. His hand goes onto her knee, and he leans over to gently kiss her on the mouth. She glances back towards the house like she's terrified I'll see them, and although I can't see Grant's face now, I'm pretty sure he's laughing at her paranoid behaviour. He's confident I won't watch him from the window. He thinks I won't break his rules.

I wait for them to pull away before heading into Ella's room. Our three-year-old daughter is sleeping soundly like she always does. I smile, gently stroking a finger down her button nose. I love her so much, and that's why I have to get out of here. For her.

CHAPTER TWO

MAVERICK

Today is Fun Day. I hate this shit, but it's necessary if we want to get the locals on our side. While my dad thought I was on an adventure travelling the country, I was actually doing research. I stopped by a lot of MC clubs to find ways to make our MC more successful. I hated the way Dad ran it, and although he'd cleaned it up over the years, mainly because associates stopped using the club, he had no interest in making us bigger or more successful. We could rake the cash in with the right direction, and that's the way I plan to run things. So today, we're opening the club up to the general public as a way to build trust.

I look around the yard at the bouncy castles and ball pits we had set up for the kids. That's something we're also missing at the club—good relationships. Only one of our older members has an ol' lady. Gears claimed Diamond back in the beginning, and they had two sons, Ghost and Scar, who are also club members. Other than Gears, the guys remained single. Scar once claimed a woman who hated the club, had his kid, and remained outside of the club. Scar hardly sees his teenage daughter. Others have kids who are now grown, and most are part of the club, but that's where the line stops. Our younger guys are too busy fucking whores to settle down, and that needs to stop too, or we'll never continue our line.

"Isn't this lovely?" gushes Mum, joining me.

"It would be better if half the local police force hadn't turned up," I mutter.

"Grim's right on that, we need to have them on side." It started because Grim invited a cop who's taken an interest in hassling us. He doesn't look like the type to change his opinion of us.

"Pres, the Taylors have arrived," announces Dice in my ear.

I take a deep breath and paste a smile on my face. The Taylors are one of the scariest motherfucking gangs around here, and I wanna do business with them. Arthur, the head of the family, stands with his three brothers, Albert, Charlie, and Tommy. They all look the part, mobsters with neat haircuts and smart suits. "Arthur," I greet, shaking his hand. "Glad you could make it."

"You didn't mention half of London's police force were coming," he says dryly.

"Yeah, well, part of my plan to conquer the world."

The gates open, pulling my attention to Officer Carter, the cop who's been watching my club a little too closely. But it isn't him I'm watching. Beside him is the most beautiful woman I've ever seen. She's flawless, with curves in all the right places. Her bright blue eyes dart around nervously as she clings to his arm. On his other side, he holds the hand of a little girl. She's just as beautiful as her mum, and her blue eyes are piercing as she looks around with delight.

"Head on inside. I'll meet you in there so we can discuss some things," I tell Arthur. He nods curtly and leads his family away. "Officer Carter," I say, smiling bitterly, "you made it." I catch the woman's eye for the briefest second before she lowers her gaze to the ground. "Is your annoying colleague coming too?"

"She'll be here," he grunts out, equally displeased to speak to me.

"Aren't you gonna introduce us to your hot wife?" comes Grim's voice, and Carter looks fit to explode.

"Show some respect," he warns.

"My bad." Grim smirks. "Lady Carter, I'm Grim, and this is my President, Maverick. Pleasure to make your acquaintance," he drawls in his best posh accent.

His wife keeps her head lowered as she peeks at Grim through her eyelashes, and I think I spot a small smile. "When you're done flirting with my wife," hisses Carter.

"Go and have some fun," I cut in. "There's plenty for the kid to do, and a food and drink stand."

I watch them walk off into the crowd. "That's weird," says Grim. "She must be hot in that clothing."

I nod in agreement. Her long-sleeved sweater and jeans aren't the sort of outfit for today's heat. Carter keeps a hold of the little girl, not encouraging her to go off and play like the other parents here. Grim slaps my shoulder, pulling my attention. "Come on, we have a meeting to attend."

∞

Arthur plays the part of head mobster well. He gives nothing away as I lay my plans on the line. Occasionally, he nods once to show he's listening, but other than that, he's still and serious.

"Why now?" asks Tommy. He seems to have adopted the role of right-hand man to his older brother.

"Eagle lost ties with any past associates," I explain. Arthur smirks, knowing everyone the club did business with cut ties after Dad fucked up so much. "It left the club in a mess. I've hidden a lot of it from the brothers, but there's no way I can drag us out of the debt he built up. We have to go back to old ways to build a new life," I say honestly, because there's no point in sugar coating it. I've cleared out what little money my dad had in the club's account to pay off some of his smaller debts, and I've used my own money to pay for the new furniture to give the place a bit of life.

"Why would I use your men when I can employ my own?" Arthur asks, steepling his fingers against his chin.

"Cos I'm in charge now and I plan to run things differently. I'm not asking to be involved in the criminal side, although we're happy to supply manpower if you need it. But a protection racket could bring us both a lot of money around here. It's open for us to step right in. We clear out the crackheads, then if you choose to supply in the area, that's your call. We don't want in on that. The rundown bars in the area need security, and that we can do."

"Together, we can rule this area," adds Grim.

Arthur sniggers. "I don't need you for that. If I wanted to expand, I could take this area no problem. The way I see it, you're offering a half-decent proposition for something I could do on my own."

I sigh. "I want to form an alliance. I'm offering up this area to split with you."

"At the cost of associating our family name with your club?" asks Charlie, rolling his eyes. It's true, the club's lost the fear factor, and I need this association with the Taylors to build up our reputation again. Not only does that stop other MCs from taking over the area, but it also opens new doors and new connections.

Grim stands abruptly, and I see Charlie press his hand to his waistband. "We're getting nowhere. If you don't wanna partner, then get the fuck gone. We have shit to deal with." I wince at his harsh words. The last thing we need is this family as our enemy.

"I didn't say I wasn't interested, relax yourself," Arthur drawls. "Your terms need tweaking."

"Our terms are staying. There is no tweaking," snaps Grim.

"You want a fifty-fifty split on any profits. I will agree to thirty-seventy for us."

I scoff, shaking my head. "Forty-sixty."

Arthur exchanges a glance with Tommy before nodding once and standing. He reaches out a hand, and I shake it. "We'll be in touch."

They breeze out of the office, and I slump back in my chair. I'm not used to this wheeling and dealing. "I can't believe you spoke to him like that," I mutter in disbelief. Grim often makes me cringe with his bluntness, but it's why he makes a good VP.

"The guy's a dick. He ain't better than us cos he wears a fucking expensive suit. Arthur Taylor grew up in the poorest parts of Peckham, he should remember his roots."

"We gotta keep them on side, Grim. We don't have a choice. He's gonna throw scraps of work our way, and we have to take it without a grumble. He's gonna test our loyalty until he trusts us. You gotta keep your mouth under control."

"Brother, I ain't bowing down to no man. Neither should you. He'll think you're weak."

"Right now," I rub my brow, "I am. The more shit I uncover, the weaker I am. My old man screwed this place over, so if I have to beg at the feet of Arthur fucking Taylor, it's because I don't have a choice."

"And now, we have to break the news to the guys." Grim heads for the door.

"And for the love of fucking God, will you just call me 'Pres'."

"Never," he throws over his shoulder as he leaves. It's becoming a running joke. We've been friends for far too long, and he refuses to address me as 'President' like the other guys have to.

Nelly sticks her head around my office door. "Can I have a word?"

"Sure."

"You know how I told you about my neighbour?" she asks, and I nod. "Well, he's here. He's here with his family."

"And does she look scared or battered?"

Nelly shakes her head. "But that doesn't mean anything, right? She could just be good at hiding it."

"Would this guy really be ballsy enough to show her off in front of his fellow officers?"

Nelly shrugs. "It's just a feeling I have."

"Go and talk to them. Befriend them as a neighbour and see if you get the same bad vibes. And we're in a place full of cops, so go tell someone if you're that worried."

RYLEE

I was surprised when Grant announced this little outing. We're new to this area and it's important he gets to know his colleagues. Plus, his boss encouraged all the officers to show up, because they think this gang is up to no good. Some of the other cops were bringing their families, and Grant loves to play the part of a loving family man.

Of course, there were rules before we left. Don't look at another man. Don't speak unless spoken to. Cover up. Wear plenty of makeup to hide my drab and dreary face, his words not mine. I also had to warn Ella to be on her best behaviour. No crying and no running off to play. We have an appearance to keep up and we'll both be in big trouble if we show him up.

Grant's partner, Lois, arrives alone. I didn't expect her to be married, as she looks younger than us. She greets us with warmth, smiling brighter when she greets Grant. I watch them closely, the way they smirk at each other while throwing banter back and forth. Their eyes gleam for one another, and it makes me sick. Grant's always had other women on the side, but he still refuses to let me go. I'm jealous that she gets to see this side of him while I get the monster.

He kisses me on the head. "I have to speak to Lois about something. Stay here," he orders. I nod, and he catches my eye to give me that look, the one that tells me he means this exact spot. I take Ella's hand and watch him disappear with Lois.

"Mama, can I play on the bouncy castle?" asks Ella. She knows I'm weak for her pleas, but I can't let her play. If Grant sees her, I'll pay dearly for it. I shake my head, and she looks sad. It breaks my heart.

"Hey," comes a female voice, and I turn to find a woman around my age, smiling brightly. "I'm Nelly."

I glance around, but there's no sign of Grant or his lover. I clear my throat, it's a nervous habit. "Rylee."

"And who is this cutey?" asks Nelly, crouching to Ella.

"Ella," I reply.

"Doesn't she want to go and play with the other kids?"

I tug Ella closer to me. "She's fine."

Nelly stands back up and eyes me for a second. "I think I live next door to you."

It catches me off guard, and the urge to run is overwhelming. "I haven't managed to see anyone yet. It's been full on, moving here."

"Umm, I've seen your husband a lot. He's a cop, right?" I nod. "Do you want a drink or anything?" she asks, and I shake my head. "Oh, come on, I work the bar, so I can get us a freebie."

I look around again, still not seeing any sign of Grant. "I'm fine here," I insist.

"I might be out of line here, but my gut is telling me to say something, so I'm just gonna do it, and if I'm wrong, we'll probably laugh about it when we become great friends." She pauses, and my heartbeat begins to speed up. "I hear you sometimes. Most of the time, actually. I recognise the screams because I've been there, and I want to help, but I'm not sure if you want that or . . ."

My breathing is shallow and my eyes dart around, looking for an escape. "I don't know what you're talking about," I mutter.

"I know someone who can help," she says desperately.

I shake my head. "I'm fine." I march off in the direction I saw Grant go, pulling Ella along with me.

Stepping inside the large warehouse-type building, I breathe a sigh of relief. I wasn't expecting that confrontation and I handled it badly. As I look around frantically for Grant, a shadow falls over me. I look up into the eyes of the man who greeted us outside, Maverick is how Grant addressed him. He smiles, and my breath catches in my throat. Everything about this man screams alpha, and lord knows I've had enough of that in my life. But something about him brings blush to my cheeks.

"You lost?" he asks, and I shake my head. "Your man was heading for the bathroom last time I saw him. Been there a while, though."

I glance towards the bathroom. Going in there would be stupid, because I know what I'll find, but standing here with this man is just as stupid. If Grant sees me, I don't know what he'll do.

"Thank you." I step in that direction, and Maverick grabs my wrist. I automatically flinch, and he drops it instantly. He looks mortified, but I smile to hide the fact I'm terrified of my own damn shadow.

"I just think it's a bad idea to go in there," he says quietly.

I'm lost in his eyes for a second, so when I hear my name being called, I don't instantly respond. It isn't until Grant is in my face that I snap out of it. "Sorry," I mutter. "Ella needed the toilet."

Grant is angry. It's in his eyes, but he can't do anything here, so he nods stiffly. "Go."

I lead Ella towards the bathroom, leaving Grant and Maverick together. I'm shaking uncontrollably as I push open the door, and I freeze when I see Lois touching up her makeup in the mirror. She's got the 'just fucked' look. I offer a weak smile as I push Ella towards a stall, and when we step back out, she's still there. "Are you having a nice time?" she asks, and I nod, helping Ella to wash her hands. "Grant is really great," she states. "You're so lucky."

"I am," I say with a fake smile while I'm seething inside. How dare she speak to me like she's a friend when it's quite obvious she's fucking my husband?

A loud bang on the door causes me to jump in fright. "Rylee?" snaps Grant. I pull Ella behind me and leave the bathroom, not bothering to dry her hands. It'll only annoy him more if he's kept waiting. "What took so long?" he hisses.

"Sorry, Lois was talking to me." His face falters and he glances behind me like he can suddenly see through the wooden door.

Following him back outside, he squeezes my hand tightly, but I know better than to moan about it. A colleague stops us so he can speak with Grant, and I sense the irritation in his voice. He wants me alone so he can grill me about why I moved and what Maverick and I were talking about.

"Ella wants to play," I say, interrupting his conversation. Grant frowns. I've never broken his rules before, but I figure I'm going to get into serious trouble anyway, so why should Ella suffer.

He takes a deep breath, and his colleague smiles awkwardly because he doesn't understand why Grant isn't agreeing. "Isn't she tired?" he grits out.

I shake my head, and Grant pinches my wrist hard. I remain still and smile. "Nope, she's desperate to join the other kids."

Grant smirks. His eyes are alight with anger but also amusement. This is all a big game, and he doesn't understand why I'm suddenly taking part after months of being a doormat. "Could you excuse us," he asks his colleague, but I laugh, shaking my head.

"Don't be silly, darling. You finish your conversation, and I'll just be over there with Ella. Take your time." I grip Ella's hand tighter than I mean to but lead her away quickly, not daring to look back. "You can have a few minutes," I tell Ella, and she claps her hands together in excitement and rushes off.

I watch her bounce, giggling and screaming like all the other kids. She never gets to interact like this, and it breaks my heart. It'll be worth the beating I'll take for defying him like this. I'm beginning to feel like there's no way out. Grant watches my every move, and when he isn't around, he locks me in the house with no way of communicating. I have no money, no bank account, and no friends or family to help me. If I run to anyone here, I risk them not believing me, and there's no doubt in my mind, he'll kill me.

I feel Grant's presence as he appears beside me, watching our daughter. "I'm not sure if you're brave or really stupid," he murmurs.

"Pretty sure I'm both."

"For every minute you delay us going home, I'll punish you harder."

"We're in a place crawling with cops," I mutter. "What's to stop me going to them?"

"You think they'd believe you over me?" He laughs hard. "You're nothing but a fantasist. I've warned them of your illness, and you acting out here will only confirm my story. You think I'd bring you here without explaining what a nightmare you are with your mental illness? Fuck, Rylee, you have no idea how sympathetic they are about this situation that I'm trapped in."

"I don't have a mental illness," I hiss.

"You do, darling. Let's not go over it again. I know you struggle to understand it, and that's why I look after you." He wraps his arm around my waist and pulls me into his side. "Now, get Ella so we can go home. It's going to be another long night."

CHAPTER THREE

MAVERICK

I watch Carter and his wife. She's a nervous wreck. Pale, withdrawn, and tired-looking, but that still doesn't mean he's beating on her. The way she flinched earlier made me jump to crazy conclusions. For a second back there, I thought she was gonna cry. It's also very clear Carter's fucking his partner. They were in the bathroom for twenty minutes at least. Then it occurs to me— this is who Nelly is talking about. These are her neighbours.

Carter wraps his arm around her waist and tugs her to him, whispering something in her ear. She then calls her daughter's name, and they head for the exit. Something looks very wrong. Her expression is void of any emotion.

Nelly joins me, also watching the pair leave. "Well, I tried talking to her and I fucked it up."

"You were right, though, something is off, and she's scared of him," I say.

"But she's not ready to accept help."

"Keep trying. She's just scared. He must leave her alone sometimes. What about when he works? Call round, maybe she'll open up to you over time." As we watch them leave, I can't help but think time might be running out. "What's her name?"

"Rylee."

"I'll get a room set up for when she needs it. She might be our first customer." It's a plan we've only recently talked about, but helping women suffering domestic abuse is something I think the club can do. We need a focus to keep us going in the right direction.

I approach Carter's partner, Lois Grey. She eyes me with suspicion. "Does your boss know you're screwing your partner?" I ask.

Blushing, she looks around to check no one's heard. "You can't prove shit."

"Go to his house," I tell her.

"Why would I do that?"

"Just go there now and check if things are okay."

"What are you trying to say, Maverick?"

"I don't like cops, I can't even pretend to, and I'd never turn to one of you for anything, but I think you need to check on Carter's wife."

She frowns. "Rylee? Why?"

"I just have a bad feeling about your friend. I don't think Rylee is safe."

"You're way off the mark. Grant loves his family. He doesn't stop talking about them."

I laugh. "He's fucking you, and that doesn't match with the man he's portraying himself to be. What makes you think he's not a complete monster if he can lie so easily?"

She chews on her lower lip. "What would I say? I can't just turn up."

"Do a drive-by. Just check it's all quiet."

"Fine, but if you're wrong about this . . ."

"What if I'm right?"

※

Grim chugs back a beer. "You sure this is worth it?" he asks. When it's clear I have no clue what he's talking about, he tips his bottle towards the groups of people milling around the yard. "Having all these people here. I don't see any fucker interacting with a biker."

"We didn't do it to make friends. I want the locals to relax around us. If they get to trust us, even a little, they won't be pointing the finger in our direction every time shit goes down. We're gonna clean the streets up, and once they see that, they'll trust us."

"And then what?"

"And then we'll be able to work alongside the mafia and keep the peace with the locals. We'll put money back into the community. They'll be grateful for the MC, and then we're unstoppable."

※

I repeat the same lines from earlier in church to the brothers. I can tell by the scowl on Crow's face that he ain't happy. Getting in bed with the mafia isn't something Dad would ever have done. "This is bullshit," he hisses.

"It's smart," I snap.

"We'll be their fucking bitches!"

"Partners," I correct.

"Partners take an equal cut. We're not partners, so cut the shit. We ain't stupid. You think you know the world cos you've been travelling the country while we were all here running this place. Then you walk back in and take over, make unnecessary changes, and wipe every trace of Eagle out of here."

"Fuck this," growls Grim. "Tell them the fucking truth."

I glance at some of the older members. I hate that Dad let them down, but protecting them is only causing them to mistrust my decisions. "We need this."

"Why?" demands Crow.

"There's no money. Without this alliance, we'll lose the club."

"This place is paid for," says Copper.

I shake my head. "I found the paperwork. Dad left everything in that box you told me about," I say. "Along with his funeral arrangements were debts. Lots of them. I had to pay the urgent ones, including rent on this place and that leaves nothing. He took out a re-mortgage last year! This building doesn't belong to us, it belongs to the bank!"

"You just furnished the place," snaps Crow.

"With my own money."

"I don't believe you. Eagle wouldn't have left us with nothing."

"He didn't intend on dying!" snaps Grim. "But he did, and now, we have this mess to sort out, so if you don't wanna support us in this, you know where the door is." The room falls silent. "That goes for anyone else. We're trying our best here, and I trust Mav with my life. If he says this is the way forward, then it is."

Copper nods in agreement. "You're right. Well done, Pres. Good call."

RYLEE

I can't breathe. Water fills my mouth and nose, and I try to hold my breath, but it's too long. When Grant eventually pulls me from the cold water, I gasp so hard, I cough and splutter, spraying water everywhere. He shoves me hard, and I land in a heap on the floor. Blood drips from my mouth and mixes with the water, spreading across the white tiles. He makes a grab for my hair, but there's a knock at the door. Relief floods me.

"Stay fucking quiet," he hisses, fastening his trousers. I nod. He disappears, and I grab the nearest towel, pressing it to my bloody lip.

Carefully, I creep out onto the landing and listen. Grant is laughing, and I can hear a female voice that sounds like Lois. "It's a misunderstanding," he explains. "Come on, all couples argue."

"It's just . . . the neighbour reported hearing screams," she says. "Can you get your wife for me?"

"Lois, this is me," he argues, but I hear the worry in his tone.

"Isn't it best I'm here and not one of the other guys?" Lois asks. "We can sort this out between us, but I need to see she's okay."

They're whispering, but it's too quiet for me to hear exactly what they're saying, and then it sounds like they're kissing. I roll my eyes. This stupid bitch isn't gonna save me. She's probably the type to think she'll be the one to change him . . . just like I once did.

I head back into the bathroom and pull the plug from the bath, releasing the copper-tinted water. I look in the mirror, assessing my bruised lip. The rest of the damage is to my body, in places I can hide. Suddenly, the door swings open and Grant pushes his face into mine. "My partner wants to do a welfare check on you. Some of the neighbours told her they heard your fucking screaming."

"I'm sorry," I mutter.

He pinches my chin in his fingers and inspects my lip. "You fell in the bathroom and split it. Understand?" I nod. "Rylee, if you say anything, I'll kill you. You don't want Ella growing up without a mother, do you?" I shake my head. "No one can protect you from me."

He takes my hand and leads me towards the bedroom. "Won't be a second," he calls down to Lois. "She's just gotta get dressed." He shoves some joggers and a baggy jumper into my arms and watches as I pull them on. "I think this time was it," he says, staring at my stomach. He decided today that we're gonna have another child, and so, not only did he force himself on me, but he didn't use protection.

He kisses me hard, biting my lip as he pulls away, and I wince. "Be a good girl and I'll treat you." I nod. By treat, he means he'll let me sit beside him tonight instead of on the floor. Like I fucking want to be anywhere near him.

I take a deep breath and follow him down into the lounge. Lois smiles, then narrows her eyes on my lip. "Everything okay?"

I nod. "Yeah."

"You sure? Someone said they heard screaming."

"Not me," I say, shrugging.

"What happened to your lip?"

"I slipped in the bathroom."

She smirks. "Of course, you did. Look, what's going on?"

"As you can see, she's fine, Lois," snaps Grant.

"Only she isn't, is she?"

"Look, I didn't want to say because I was embarrassed, what with you fucking my husband, but I did this during sex," I blurt out, and Grant stiffens beside me. "I like it a little rough and I banged my lip on the headboard. But I guess you know how he gets," I say, and Lois blushes. "Now, if you'll excuse me." I rush off upstairs, slamming the bedroom door to wait for his angry footsteps.

It's hard to get comfortable, but I carefully lay my head down on the couch. Grant left for work less than ten minutes ago, and I had to get up and pretend I was fine even though my ribs are screaming in pain and it hurts to take in a breath. A gentle tap at the front door makes me groan. I can't get up, and I'm not allowed to answer it anyway. Besides, Grant has the keys with him.

The letterbox lifts and a female voice floats through the opening. "Rylee, hi, it's me, Nelly." I stay quiet. She can't see me. "I know you're hurt. I heard you well into the night. I tried to tell that cop about it when she stopped by yesterday, but she told me she'd seen you and you were fine." I roll my eyes. Grant had taken a good half-hour to return after I'd left them alone. Then, he spent the next few hours torturing me. "Please answer me. I just want to know you're okay. I've got you some strong painkillers." She pushes a pill packet through the letterbox.

"Ella," I whisper, and she looks up from her doll. "Go and get Mummy those pills." She does as I ask, smiling at Nelly through the small gap in the door.

"Hi, Ella. Is Mummy okay?"

Ella looks over to me, unsure of how to answer. "I'm fine," I grate out.

"Let me help," Nelly begs.

I push myself to sit, groaning in pain. "You can't help me. Ella, come here and play with your doll." She hands me the pills, and I swallow two without water. Grant refuses to give me any pain medication. He prefers that I suffer.

"That's what he wants you to think, Rylee, but I *can* help. There's protection out there for you. I've found you a safe place."

"I'll never be safe."

"I've been there. I was like you, and trust me, there is help."

"He's a cop. He'll make my life hell."

"I'll stand by you every step of the way."

"You don't even know me," I almost wail. "Why would you help me?"

"Because I know what it's like to feel so fucking alone. He's done that! He's made you think no one will believe you, but what have you got to lose by letting me help? He's gonna beat you regardless, so let me at least try."

I've never had anyone offer to help. "I don't have anything. No money, no bank account."

"I'll help you."

"He'll take Ella."

"He won't. I'll keep you both safe."

"How?"

"My friends have a safe place. They're trying to help people just like you. If you agree, they'll get you out of there, keep you safe, and even give you work."

"Why would they do that?" It seems too good to be true.

"Why question it? You need the help, and I'm offering it to you. Please, let me help you. Things can't be worse than here, can they?"

Moving to the door, I stare at Nelly through the letterbox. "He said he'd kill me."

"Sweetie, if you stay here, he'll do that eventually anyway. Let me make that call."

I take a deep breath before nodding. She's right . . . I have nothing else to lose.

CHAPTER FOUR

MAVERICK

We approach the food counter, and an older man glares at us. "You the boss around here?" Grim asks.

"What if I am?"

I turn my back on the counter and stare at the group of youths. They look the same age as the twins and they're ready for a fight. "We just wanted to leave a message," continues Grim. This rundown café is the epicentre for most of the drugs in this area. Youths collect the packages here and go out delivering, returning in the evening with their money. We can't allow it anymore because Arthur needs the patch for his own drugs.

"And what's that?" asks the man, folding his arms across his chest.

"We're putting an end to your business on the streets," I say, turning back to face him. He frowns. "The only business you've got here from today is food. Nothing else will be leaving these premises."

"What the fuck are you talking about?" he snaps.

There's a thud from the back where Lock, Dice, and Crow have kicked the door in. The man rushes to see what's going on, and I turn back to the group. "You hear that? No more dealing from here, boys, so run along."

"You can't tell us what to do!" spits out one of the kids.

The noise of my guys breaking shit out back gets louder. "Who the hell are you?" asks another kid.

"We're The Perished Riders MC," Grim grins, "and we're taking over these streets. You need work, you come to us." He throws a business card onto a nearby table. "There's real money to be made, and you ain't gonna go to prison for it."

We step out into the street just as my phone rings out. "Nelly?" I answer.

"Pres, I need your help to get into a house."

"What makes you think I can help with that?" I ask, throwing my leg over my bike.

"It's a rescue mission. I'm with Rylee, and she needs our help."

I don't need to be told twice. "Send me the address. I'm on my way."

Ten minutes after receiving Nelly's call, we stop outside the address Nelly sent. She's kneeling at the door, looking through the letterbox. I turn to Crow, who's been breaking and entering since he was eight years old. "Can you get that door open?"

"You want me to break into a cop's house?" he asks, and I nod. "Christ," he mutters, opening his tail bag and pulling out the tool he needs to pick the lock.

"She's really scared," says Nelly. "He's told her he'll always find her, and that he'll kill her."

"It's what they all say. We'll protect her. Hadley is a lawyer—she'll get the right paperwork in place."

Crow has the door open in minutes. I pat him on the back, and for a second, I think he almost smiles. When the door is fully open, the little girl I met yesterday stares wide-eyed at the group of bikers on her doorstep. "Hey, you, do you remember me?" I ask, lowering to one knee so I'm at her level, and she nods. "I've come to take you and your mum on an adventure." She smiles. "Have you ever been on a motorbike?" I ask, and she shakes her head. "Well, as it's your first time, we'd better make it super special. I'll let you choose whose bike you want to ride on." She points to me, and Grim laughs. I've never been great with kids, but for this one, I'll try.

I head inside and find Nelly helping Rylee from the couch. She's in a bad way and covered in bruises. "Fuck," I mutter. "I don't know if you'll be okay on a bike."

"I'll put her on the front of mine," says Grim, but something inside me feels the urge to protect this woman with my life. I shake my head.

"I'll take her. You'll take the kid."

"Whatever you say," he agrees and goes to speak to the kid.

"I'm gonna lift you. Just hold on to my neck, and I'll do the rest." I scoop her up, and she cries out, burying her face into my neck and wrapping her arms around me. "Sorry," I whisper. I carefully carry her to my bike and throw my leg over, keeping her in my arms while I get comfortable. "Keep your arms there. I'm gonna sit you on the tank and keep you side on like this." She nods and does exactly as I say. Starting the bike, I straighten up and fit her nicely across my legs. "Take one last look," I tell her, "cos you ain't ever gonna come back here."

Diamond, Gears's ol' lady, steps from the bedroom where I laid Rylee half an hour ago. She's a nurse, which works out well for the club cos there's always someone needing medical help. "Is she okay?" I ask.

"I suspect broken ribs, a lot of them. She needs a scan to be sure they aren't causing internal damage."

"We can't take her to the hospital. They'll record it, and he'll come looking."

"Right," she says and sighs. "Let me call in a favour. I know a private place that carries out abortions. They'll have a scanner we can use." I kiss her on the head gratefully. "One more thing—she's asked for the morning after pill. I think he raped her . . . more than once, by the sounds of it."

I squeeze my hands into fists. That piece of shit needs to pay.

I step into the room. Rylee is laid on top of the bedsheets as still as a statue, staring up at the ceiling. Her skin is porcelain pale and there's dark circles around her eyes. Her lips are dry and split, and there's bruising around her neck. It shows how much makeup she wore on the Fun Day—she looked so radiant then. "Diamond is gonna have you scanned. She's worried about your ribs."

"They usually heal well," she croaks out.

"Well, we ain't taking no chances. Are you feeling okay, apart from the obvious?"

A tear leaks from the corner of her eye. "What if he finds me?" she whispers.

"He'll need to get through at least fifteen bikers to get to you. You're safe here."

"Why are you helping me?"

"Let's just say I'm making up for past mistakes."

RYLEE

Maverick leaves, and I frown. What did he mean by that? Did he hurt his wife? I swipe away my tears. Nelly took Ella so I could rest, but I'm feeling anxious without her. Ella is always with me. I start to cry again, because all I seem to do is cry.

The door opens and a younger girl comes in. "Hi, I'm Meli."

"Hi."

"I'm Mav's sister. I just wanted to come in and tell you Ella's fine. My twin, Hadley, is with her. She's great with kids. Do you need anything?"

I shake my head. "Why is Maverick helping me?" It's playing on my mind.

She smiles, shrugging her shoulders. "He's weird. He gets ideas, and somehow, everyone just goes along with it. Mum thinks he's holding some guilt, but who knows. Mav's hard to work out."

"Guilt for what?"

"Past stuff with our parents." I feel relieved by her confession, at least he hasn't beaten his wife. "He never lies. If he's told you he'll help, he will. You're safe now, Rylee."

∞

Maverick arranges for me to go to a private clinic to have a scan of my ribs. It's all a little cloak and dagger, as I'm driven in a car with blacked-out windows flanked by motorbikes. Nelly comes too, and makes a joke about feeling like the Queen, but I'm too terrified to see the humour.

I'm led in through a back door and straight into a room with a scanner. A doctor smiles warmly, inviting me to lie down on the bed. Nelly stays nearby, holding Ella, who seems to have taken a shine to her. Diamond watches as the doctor scans my sore ribs. "There's six broken ribs on your left side," he confirms, "but with plenty of rest, they'll heal fine." He eyes the window, where a few bikers are pacing outside the room. "If you need help—" he begins.

Diamond laughs. "You're barking up the wrong tree there, Doc. This wasn't them. They're the reason she's safe now."

"That true?" he asks me, and I nod in response.

The door opens and Maverick sticks his head in. "We done here?" he asks as the doctor helps me to sit. "We gotta get out of here." Maverick hands the doctor a bundle of cash and takes me by the hand, leading me back towards the car.

"Everything okay?" asks Nelly.

"I'll drive the car," he says to Dice. "You take my bike back."

We get in the car, and Nelly pushes for an answer. "Mav?"

"She's all over the news," he mutters, and I catch his eye in the rear-view mirror.

"But she's not been missing long enough to warrant a news story. The cops wouldn't touch a missing person until at least twenty-four hours."

"Yeah, well, he's saying she's fucking vulnerable and needs urgent medication."

We get back to the club, but the entire journey is a blur. Every police patrol car we pass makes me want to vomit. Grant always said he'd do whatever it takes to find me if I ever tried to leave him. I know he'll kill me for this.

Nelly gets Ella out of the car, but I remain seated, my mind racing a mile a minute. Everything in me wants to run back and beg for his forgiveness. Maybe if he sees how sorry I am, he'll let me live. Maverick opens the passenger door, interrupting my thoughts and startling me. "It'll be okay."

"He'll find me. He won't stop until he does."

"I've never done this," he says. "It's new to me, so I don't know how the law works, but we'll work it all out and make sure you're safe. You don't have to stay with anyone you don't want to. He can't force you back."

"He'll make my life a living hell. Maybe I should just go back and save everyone this trouble."

He takes my hand and stares right into my eyes, and for a second, the world stops and all I see is him. "You're no trouble, Rylee. You did the hardest thing by leaving, so now, you just gotta keep moving forwards." He makes it seem so easy.

Diamond joins us. "I'm gonna get those tablets, Rylee. Do you need anything else while I'm gone?"

"Oh, erm, I have no cash," I mutter, feeling embarrassed.

"Don't sweat it. Mav's got you covered." She smiles before heading off.

"Tablets? The doc gave you something?" asks Maverick, and my blush deepens.

"It's an over-the-counter medicine. The morning-after pill," I say quietly, and something passes over his face—maybe a look of anger, though I can't be sure.

"Oh, yeah, Diamond mentioned that." He keeps hold of my hand as he helps me out of the car and leads me into the clubhouse without another word.

The large screen television hanging on the bar wall is showing the local news channel. Maverick yells at his sister to turn it off. "Am I on there?" I ask, and Hadley exchanges a worried look with Maverick. "I want to see," I insist. I need to know how bad this really is, so I turn the television back on.

Grim hands me his mobile phone. "You're everywhere." I stare in horror at the picture of me and Ella on the screen. I scroll down through the local news article. The headline reads, 'Worry for missing vulnerable mother and child.'

"What am I gonna do?" I ask.

"We're gonna meet about it and discuss the best way forward," says Mav.

"We?" I ask.

"Me and my brothers," he replies. "I'll let you know what we decide." I watch as Maverick moves towards a room where the other men are filing in.

"Can't I listen in?" I ask, and he shakes his head, disappearing inside.

Hadley smiles awkwardly. "It's kind of a rule. They call that," she points to the closed door that houses a room full of bikers, "church. They meet there to decide club stuff and vote on things. Women generally aren't allowed. Sometimes, Meli barges in there. She likes to break rules and annoy Mav."

"So, they'll make a decision about me without me?"

She shrugs. "I guess so. It sounds worse than it is. They're very old-fashioned like that. My mum used to say it's the man's job to keep us safe in the club, and it's always been the way."

I stare down at the floor, trying to process what she's saying. "The thing is, I've spent most of my life being told what to do by a man."

She winces. "I guess when you put it like that . . ."

"I'm gonna take Ella upstairs for a nap, and I'll probably join her," I say.

"You don't wanna wait around to see what Mav says?"

I shrug. "What's the point?"

CHAPTER FIVE

MAVERICK

"I knew this was a bad idea," Crow states.

"You think everything is a bad idea," mutters Copper.

"Of all the people in the fucking world to help, you pick the one woman who's got a crazy cop on her ass."

"If you ask me, it makes it even sweeter." Grim smirks. "That cop was giving us hassle."

"And when he finds out we're hiding his wife and kid here, he's gonna be just as hell-bent on taking us down."

"Enough," I snap. "I don't wanna hear your negative bullshit, Crow. Support this or fuck off. So, this cop has spun the story that Rylee is vulnerable. He's hinted in the press that she's on medication but hasn't said what for. Rylee insists she's not on any medication and is one hundred percent fit and well, apart from the obvious. We need a plan."

"First of all, she needs a job. Earning money will give her some independence," says Copper.

"Hold on a minute," Crow cuts in. "You wanna rescue these women, give them a place to live, give them jobs . . . I thought you said the club was on its knees?"

"Which brings me to the next thing. Arthur has some debts that need collecting. I need three of you to be the muscle."

"I hardly think Arthur Taylor needs any muscle," scoffs Crow.

"You're going," snaps Grim. "Just to get you out my face for a few hours."

"Good call. Crow, Ghost, and Scar, be at this address in an hour," I say, handing out a business card. "I have a meeting with Hadley, so if there's nothing else?" The guys shake their heads, so I bang the gavel, calling an end to church.

Hadley's already waiting in my office. It still feels weird sitting in my dad's office chair, but I do it anyway. That's one thing I didn't feel right replacing. "What do you need?" she asks.

Hadley took up law and is in her first year of placement. Dad pushed her to it because he fancied having a lawyer at his beck and call, but she has a natural flair for shit like this. She just knows what she's talking about. "I wanna know how I can protect Rylee from that bastard."

"Legally, he can't force her to go back to him. Our problem is, I doubt she ever filed any complaint against him, so there's no history of incidents to back up what she's saying he's done. Even the doctor she saw today did it off the record. So, it'll be really difficult to get an injunction to keep him away from her. Carter is claiming there's something vulnerable, he might say she's mentally ill and therefore can't care for herself, so I guess we just have to prepare for every eventuality."

"How?"

"We have an answer for everything he could possibly throw. Like, if he says she can't care for herself or make decisions, we list the times he left her alone with a child to care for. We should also work on making him look less credible. People will automatically listen to him because of his job, so let's start showing him for what he is."

"He's having an affair with his partner. I caught them on CCTV going in and out of the bathroom together. It's obvious what they've been doing."

"Good start. Maybe put someone on him and get more evidence of that?"

"Thanks, Hads."

"No problem." She heads to the door, then stops. "Actually, one last thing. I think Rylee felt a bit upset earlier with you guys making decisions without her."

"It wasn't like that."

"She doesn't get it, Mav. She's not from our world and she's spent years being told what to do by a man. If you wanna help, give her some control. That's important to remember when helping victims like Rylee."

I tap on Rylee's bedroom door, and after a few minutes, she opens it. "Hey," I smile, "Hadley thinks you're upset with me."

She looks mortified and steps out the room. "No, not at all."

"It's okay," I reassure her. "I get why."

"I don't want you to think I'm being ungrateful. It just felt weird you all discussing me like that."

"It was a shit move, and I should have thought about that. I'm used to just getting on with our ways and not explaining to anyone. I'll make sure I explain shit better next time. If you're free now, can we talk?"

She nods, and I wait for her to open her bedroom door. When she doesn't, I frown, causing her to blush. "It's weird being in a bedroom with another man. And Ella is sleeping."

"I have a balcony off my room. Could we sit out there and have coffee?" She nods in agreement, and we head for my room.

I've had the top floor of the clubhouse since I was a teenager. It's like a small apartment up here, with a separate bathroom, bedroom, and living space. I open the double doors that lead out onto the balcony and watch as she steps out. She's beautiful, but just like Hadley, she hides her face behind her hair an awful lot and shies away whenever I try to make eye contact. I make two coffees, then follow her onto the balcony and take a seat. Rylee stares over the railing out across London. "It's nice out here," she says.

"I like it when I need to think, although the traffic is always in the background."

"I don't mind that," she says. "I like background noise."

"Hadley said we need to prepare for a fight against your ex."

"Ex," she repeats. "Feels weird saying that." "How long have you been with him?"

"We married when I was seventeen." My eyes bug out of my head, and she smiles sadly. "He was my high school sweetheart. We met at age eleven."

"Your parents let you marry at seventeen?"

"They weren't really bothered. Too wrapped up in their own affairs."

"Do you see them?" I ask, and she shakes her head. "How long has it been going on? The violence."

She takes a deep breath. "All that time. At eleven years old, he'd do nasty things that made me feel inferior, but he first hit me when we were fifteen. He said I was flirting with a male teacher. I wasn't. It wasn't all the time. It's been worse since we had Ella."

"I can't imagine being with somebody for so long. It must be hard walking away,

despite him being a prick."

"I hate him. I've hated him since the day I married him. He raped me repeatedly that day," she mutters, and there's bitterness in her tone. "I just couldn't get away. At first, he'd do things like hide my passport, take my mobile. Eventually, it was easier to give those things up rather than argue every time he took them. It was such a gradual thing, giving up my control, that I didn't realise it had happened. Not until I'd had Ella, but by then, I was completely powerless."

"That will never happen to you again."

"Why are you doing this?" she asks.

"My dad wasn't very nice to my mum. I guess I always felt helpless then, but now, not so much. Most MCs support charities or help where they can, and I want this club to do exactly that. We're redecorating the rooms on your floor, and we'll open them up to people who need help. I've been in touch with the Women's Aid charity, and we're gonna raise money for them."

She smiles. "That's really great. Not many men would be this passionate."

"I don't have a clue what I'm doing," I admit with a small laugh. "I just know I wanna make this club better than what Dad did. Maybe once you're feeling up to it, you can help us. You'll be able to advise us better than anyone how we can make women feel safe."

"I'd like that," she says.

"So, back to business." She takes a seat and waits for me to continue. "We need to tell your ex you're safe." Her face fills with panic, and I reach across the table and place my hand over hers. "It's okay. I'll be right by your side. We'll use a burner phone, which means he won't trace it. You just have to tell him you're safe and you're not going back to him. That way, the local news will stop reporting on it."

She shakes her head, withdrawing her hand from my grasp. "I can't . . . I can't do that."

"You can, Rylee. You're strong. I've arranged for a support worker from Women's Aid to come and see you. We can make that call while she's here with you, and she's happy to call the police and let them know you're not a missing person and you don't require their help. The police won't follow it up if they know the charity is now supporting you. We need those kinds of witnesses."

She sucks in a breath. "He just has a way of making me do what he says," she mumbles. Her hands are clasped in front of her, but I can see them shaking.

"You don't have to listen to him. You say your piece and you disconnect." I take her hand again. "I'll be right there the whole time. He can't hurt you anymore."

RYLEE

The next day, Maverick calls me into his office. There's a woman sitting with him, and she smiles kindly as she shakes my hand. "I'm Collette. I'm a support worker for Women's Aid. I'm here to see how you're doing."

I feel myself shaking as I take the seat beside her. "I'll let you talk," says Maverick, passing to leave. I grab his hand and stop him. It shocks us both, and we stare for a second at where our hands join.

"Stay," I whisper, my eyes reaching his. "I'd like you to stay." He nods once and takes his seat again. "I feel like I'm in a dream," I say to her. "None of this feels real."

"That's to be expected. Maverick tells me you have a little girl?"

I nod. "Ella. She's three."

"Is she in school?" I shake my head. Grant didn't like the idea of her going to school, and seeing as she's legally able to stay home until five, he said we had to wait. Personally, I think it was the thought of me being out of the house he didn't like.

"Rylee is going to call him today to tell him she's left him," says Maverick.

"It's a good idea to tell him. It's the next major step in your journey."

"It makes me feel sick to my stomach, the thought of talking to him. I'm scared," I admit.

"Of course, you are. I can make that call for you if it makes it easier," she offers, "but sometimes, women find it helps them gain back a little control over the perpetrator."

I nod, because as terrified as I am, I know he needs to hear this from me.

Maverick hands me a small mobile phone. It's not a smartphone, more like an older mobile, and I take it with trembling fingers. I know Grant's number by heart. He drilled it into me years ago, not that I ever needed it in more recent years seeing as he took my phone away from me. I take a deep breath and press it to my ear.

"Yeah?" Grant barks when he answers.

"It's me," I mutter.

Collette rubs my arm and gives me an encouraging smile. "Rylee?" He gasps, sounding surprised and worried. "Where are you?"

"I'm safe, Grant. I'm just calling you to say I'm safe."

"Sorry, what?" He gives a small laugh like he can't believe what he's hearing, and I brace myself for his rage. Instead, he calmly says, "Baby, tell me where you are, and I'll come and get you. We can talk about whatever it is that's upsetting you."

"No."

"What do you mean no? Are you being held against your will?"

"Not anymore," I say. "I've left you. I'm not coming home."

"Hold on." I hear a door open and close, and suddenly, his politeness a second ago makes sense—someone was in the room with him. "Now, listen to me, Rylee. You tell me where you are right now cos I swear to God, I'll find you anyway, and when I do, I'll fucking kill you!"

"We're over," I say, feeling a little braver. "I'm never coming back." Those words feel good.

"Don't talk shit. Of course, you're coming back. What are you doing for money? How are you taking care of Ella? You're not well, Rylee, and you need me to help you."

"I have to go now."

"No!" he yells. "Don't hang up!" I hesitate. "Don't do this. I love you. I'm sorry. I can get help."

"It's too late."

"No, don't say that, baby, don't say that. We can make it work. I'll do whatever you want." My eyes water. I'd have given anything to hear these words once upon a time, but now, they feel empty and worthless.

Maverick reaches forward, taking the phone from me and turning it off. I wipe my eyes on my sleeve. I don't know why I'm feeling so upset. "He won't change," says Maverick.

I nod. "I know that. I think I feel in control for once and I don't know what to do with that."

"You did really well," says Collette. "This is your new beginning. Yours and Ella's." She hands me a box. "We put together a gift box of things you and Ella might need. We're here to support you. Maverick has my number, and you can call anytime. We have a safehouse should you need it, and we can help with all kinds of other things, such as the court process." I take the box and cry harder. It feels overwhelming. *I'm safe. I'm safe.* I repeat the mantra in my head.

Collette leaves, and while Maverick sees her out, I pull myself together. He returns and takes my hand. He seems to do that a lot. Gently pulling me to stand, he wraps his arms around me. For a minute, I freeze. It feels wrong having another man touch me at all, even in a friendly way, but as I relax against his hard chest, I breathe in his heady scent of leather and musky aftershave, and for the first time in a long time, I actually feel safe. "You were so fucking brave today, Rylee. So brave."

"I didn't feel very brave," I mumble.

"Are you kidding? You told him straight. When was the last time you took control like that and told him?"

I smile into his chest. "Never. Well, not without punishment."

"We've just gotta sit tight now and see what his next move is. I can't imagine we'll be lucky enough to just have him slope off and never bother you again." Maverick releases me, and I feel the loss immediately. "I've gotta go out. Will you be okay?" I nod. "Nelly is in today. She'll keep you company."

"The police knocked on my door," says Nelly, handing me a coffee. "I told them what an arsehole Grant was to you, but to be honest, they didn't look interested and said if you needed to make a complaint, you should get in touch yourself. I said I didn't know where you were. I told Mav, and he said you called Grant today and told him you'd left." I nod in response. "That's amazing! Well done!"

"How did you escape it?" I ask. "Who helped you?"

"My situation was different," says Nelly. "For a start, I don't have kids. I just had to worry about myself. And secondly, my ex was abusive when he was drunk. All the other times, he was so kind and loving, you wouldn't have believed it was the same man."

"So, you just left?"

"Pretty much. I gave him way too many chances and I couldn't take it anymore, so I left. He didn't care enough to hunt me down, and I should imagine he's drunk himself silly since."

"Were you with him long?"

"Two years. I left him a few months ago."

"You've done well to have your own place and a job."

"I rent the place. I have a couple of great friends who have helped me out. I'm lucky to have support. Do you have friends or family around?"

I shake my head. "I met him really young, so he kind of quashed any friendships, convinced me I only needed him. My parents aren't around here. They live in Southampton, so I don't see them."

"Maybe we could get in touch with them," she suggests.

"Maybe one day. I'd like to know what they're doing these days, whether they're still together. Dad used to hit my mum, so they might have separated."

"And friendship is definitely something we can fix. You already have me, and I can introduce you to some great people."

Maverick's mum joins us at the bar. She hasn't spoken to me yet, but I've seen her watching from a distance. Hadley told me their dad died recently, and her mum is struggling with it. "I'm Brea," she says in an Irish accent.

"Rylee."

"Sorry I haven't introduced myself sooner. I'm not usually rude. I didn't know what to say. Mav told me about your ex."

"Right," I say, unsure of what else I can add.

"And I wanted you to know I think you're so brave."

I blush. Everyone keeps telling me I'm brave, but I don't feel it. "Thanks."

"I wish I was as brave as you. I could have saved myself a world of pain."

"Sorry to hear about your husband," I offer, and she smiles sadly.

"No one understands why I'm so upset when Eagle treated me so badly, but I still loved him. I know he loved me too deep down. He was just hurting so badly, and he couldn't move past things."

"It's hard for others to understand when they're not there. I know people want to ask me why I couldn't get away, but they wouldn't understand the fear I felt."

"Mav will take care of you now. He's a good boy."

"I'm really grateful," I say. "Without his and Nelly's help, I wouldn't have been able to escape."

Suddenly, Meli rushes in with Grim on her tail. "Leave me alone," she screams.

"I can't do that."

"I'm actually starting to think you're obsessed with me," she hisses, and he scoffs.

"Please, you behave like a child. A spoiled one at that."

I spot Hadley watching the pair with interest. She's very quiet, but whenever Grim is around, something in her changes. She sits a little taller and watches his every move. I can see why—he's good-looking. In fact, most of the guys here are.

"Then get off my back. Everywhere I turn, you're there."

"If you could be trusted, I wouldn't need to follow you."

"It's been weeks since I went out," she argues.

"Leave h-h-her a-a-alone!" We all look towards the owner of the deep voice, a man sitting hunched near the bar. His hood is pulled up, hiding his face from view. He's huge. His biceps bulge through his shirt and his shoulders are wide, making me think he's stocky and tall in build.

"Fuck me, Scar. We never hear you speak and you choose now to do it!" says Grim. "I could always transfer babysitting duties to you."

"I don't need babysitting," hisses Meli.

"Enough," says Brea. "Grim, you're relieved for today. I'll watch her. She knows better than to sneak out on my watch."

"Fine, but you can tell Mav," says Grim, stalking off.

"Let's have a girls' night," Brea suggests. "It'll be a chance for us to get to know Rylee, and I need cheering up."

Meli smiles and kisses her on the cheek. "I love that idea, Mama B."

CHAPTER SIX

MAVERICK

Tommy Taylor slaps the arse of a passing waitress, and she flutters her eyelashes in his direction. He's like a walking hard-on, all testosterone and flirting. Who am I kidding? Up until a few months ago, that was me. Since taking over the club, my life's been one big ball ache. I sip my vodka and take in my surroundings. The Taylors own a string of nightclubs and up-market bars, and this one is where they do most of their business dealings. "When was the last time you got fucked, Mav? You're more uptight than a nun's arse." Charlie grins.

"Seems like forever," I say. "Shit's been complicated."

"That's never an excuse to go celibate."

"Maybe that pretty little brunette we heard about has caught your eye?" asks Arthur, and I narrow my eyes.

"How do you know about that?" I snap.

"Relax, Crow told us when he came out on the collections." I make a mental note to kick Crow's arse for discussing club business.

"We're keeping it quiet, so I'd appreciate your discretion," I mutter.

"Of course. We're partners, right?" asks Arthur, and I nod. "I don't gossip."

"She's all over the news anyway," says Albert.

"Not anymore, we sorted it." Since Rylee spoke to Grant earlier today, her story has gradually been pulled from the news.

"Maybe you should put a story out there about what that shithead did to her," Arthur suggests.

"Fuck me, Crow really opened up," whispers Grim from beside me. "I'll gut the fucker."

Arthur clicks his fingers and a group of women approaches. "Take care of my friends," he says, rising to his feet. "And you," he says, grabbing the hand of one, "can take care of me." He leads her away, leaving us with the others.

My eyesight blurs and I blink a few times as I reach in my pocket for cash to pay the taxicab. Grim steps out, taking the hands of the two ladies we've brought back to the club. I press a bunch of notes in the driver's hand and follow them.

Music pumps out from inside the clubhouse, and I frown. "Since when did we agree to a party?"

Grim opens the door. "Well, shit," he mutters, stepping inside.

I glare at the women in my life as they dance in the centre of the room. Even Mum is waving her hands around. Rat, the club's prospect, rushes over. "Thank Christ, you're back. These women are crazy."

"What are we celebrating?" I ask.

"Freedom, life, love, kids ... the list is endless. They've toasted to at least ten things."

My eyes fall to Rylee and my breath catches in my throat. Her hair is swept back away from her face, tied up neatly on her head. She's wearing makeup—not too much but enough to give her a flawless complexion with a hint of colour to make her eyes pop. "Are you seeing this, brother?" growls Grim. I nod, unable to find the words. "Where did Hadley go?" he asks, and I pull my eyes away from Rylee.

Hadley also has her hair pulled back, and I assume they let Meli loose with the styling. She looks amazing. I remember that time Dad was so cruel to her, so I head over to her. She stops and stares at me with wide, nervous eyes. "Hads, you look fucking amazing," I say, and she breaks out into a huge grin. I wish I'd had the balls to do it back when Dad ripped into her.

"Thank you," she says, blushing.

"I just wanted to say," Rylee interrupts, flopping her hand against my chest clumsily, "thank you. For rescuing me, for helping me, and most of all," she pats my chest, "for hugging me today. You give the best hugs."

I smirk. "No problem."

Hadley moves away, and Rylee moves slightly closer, almost pushing herself against me. "If I wasn't such a mess—"

I press my finger to her lips to quiet her. "You're drunk. When was the last time you were drunk?"

"Never," she says, shrugging. "Never ever."

"Then don't finish that sentence until you're sober."

Arms encircle my waist from behind, and I glance back to see one of the girls from Arthur's club. Shit, I'd forgotten about her. "You ready, baby?" she asks, pouting slightly.

Rylee steps away, and I immediately want to tug her back to me. "Sure," I reply.

"Have a good night," says Rylee, trying hard to smile.

"You too. Drink lots of water. Sleep on your side." I kiss her on the head. It's such a natural move that I don't think about it until it's done. "Goodnight, Bandia."

"Bandia?" she repeats, smiling.

I nod. "It's my new name for you."

∞

I lie back on the bed. Skye straddles me, running her fake nails across my bare chest. I'm still wearing my jeans, but it doesn't stop her rubbing herself over me. My erection strains against the material, and I close my eyes, enjoying the feel of her. She lowers herself over me, and I take her nipple into my mouth. I need to be inside her, so I lift her from me and flip her on her back. She giggles as I brace myself above her, thrusting my tongue into her mouth.

"Jesus," hisses Grim from the balcony. "That crying is putting me off my stride. You ready to swap?"

"No," I snap. "I don't even have my jeans off."

"Come on, man, I can hear someone crying and vomiting. It ain't good for the mood."

I groan, climbing from Skye and marching to the balcony. Grim's got his woman bent over the railings butt naked while he slams into her. "You look just fine to me," I mutter. He's right though, I can hear a woman crying. I look over the balcony. The windows to Rylee's room are open and it sounds like the noise is coming from there. "Fuck, I better go see if she's okay."

"I'll entertain these two ladies, brother, don't rush back." Grim winks, and I slap him on the back.

"Pres," I correct him as I head out the room.

I tap on Rylee's door, but she doesn't answer, so I carefully open it and stick my head in. "Rylee?"

There's a rustling sound followed by her panicked voice. "Don't come in."

"I just wanna check if you're okay."

"I'm fine. Honestly."

"You don't sound fine. You're crying."

"It's just . . . oh god." I don't wait for her to finish. Instead, I push the door open and go inside, then I freeze. Rylee is completely naked. It's not the sight of her perfect body that makes me stop but the sight of the bruises and old scars littering her pale skin. She's standing before the full-length mirror, staring at herself.

"Shit," I whisper, and she spins to face me, gripping her ribs in pain and flinching. "That's why you're crying?" I ask, moving closer. Her ribs are blue and green. There's boot marks on her back and bite marks across her breasts and buttocks. There's older bruises as well as more recent ones.

"I was sick," she whimpers, pointing to a pile of clothes. "I vomited on my outfit, and I got undressed and then caught my reflection in this thing," she says, pointing to the full-length mirror with disgust, like it purposely set out to expose her. "I only had a small mirror at home," she adds softly, turning back to her reflection.

"It's the first time you've seen yourself like this?" I ask, placing my hands on her shoulders and standing behind her. She nods. "They're just bruises, they'll fade," I reassure her. She sobs, covering her mouth with her hands. I turn her to me and embrace her, trying not to think about the fact she's naked and I'm shirtless. She cries against my chest, and I walk backwards to the bed, pulling back the sheets and lowering in. I tuck her under my arm, and she keeps her head rested against me, her sobs quietening.

"Is Ella okay next door?" I ask. We gave Rylee a room with a connecting door to the one next to it. That way, she could have the choice of having Ella in with her or in her own room.

"Hadley put some girly lights in there and some stickers on the wall. Ella went straight in there. She loves it."

I draw circles on her back, and she closes her eyes. "Sleep, Bandia."

"What does it mean?"

"One day, I'll tell you."

RYLEE

I sit with a start and look around the room. My head spins and I groan, feeling sick. *Sick*. I glance at the pile of clothes on the floor. I was sick . . . all over myself. I groan again and lift the sheets. I'm naked. A foggy memory of Maverick seeing me naked and crying infiltrates my brain, and I wince. Something tells me it wasn't a bad dream, but I'm alone now. I pull on a shirt and shorts and check on Ella. Her bed is empty, and I quash down my panic. She's safe here, and there's so many people helping out with her that I know she's probably downstairs with Nelly or Hadley. I head down to check, hoping to avoid seeing Maverick, since I feel ashamed and so embarrassed.

The kitchen is a hive of chatter, which only hurts my head more, but I spot Ella and instantly relax. I need a shower, so I turn to leave before I'm spotted, but I crash against a hard chest. "Going somewhere?" rumbles Maverick's deep voice. The blush burns my cheeks and I stare down at my feet, not daring to face him just yet. He lifts my chin, but I keep my eyes downcast. "Damn it, Rylee, look at me."

"I'm mortified," I whisper.

"Don't be."

"I don't usually behave like that," I explain. "I've never been drunk, and then I got sick and—" He places his finger over my lips, so I stop talking.

"Bandia, you have nothing to be ashamed of. You're perfect in every way and you trusted me enough to let me see your vulnerable side. That means a lot. Don't be embarrassed. Now, go and eat something."

"I'm not hungry," I begin, but he grips my shoulders and turns me towards the kitchen. Sitting at the head of the table, he pulls out the chair to his left, staring at me until I also sit down.

Maverick places a slice of toast on my plate. "Eat that, and I'll get off your back." I stare at it. I'm so used to hardly eating that right now, with everything going on, my appetite is non-existent. "I haven't seen you eat a thing since you arrived," he adds.

"I have eaten," I mutter. I definitely ate a banana, at least.

Grim sits to Maverick's right, a big grin on his face. "Where the hell did you end up last night?" he asks, piling his plate with eggs and bacon.

Maverick watches him fill his plate with a look of disgust. "You build up an appetite?" he asks.

"You abandoned ship," accuses a smirking Grim. "Not my fault I had to take care of them both."

"What a hardship," says Maverick dryly.

"You missed out, man."

"Pres," corrects Maverick. Out of all the people here, Grim is the only one who never seems to call him 'Pres'.

"Star passed out and left me and Skye to it. Skye could not get enough, brother. She was like a horny rabbit all night long."

I nibble on my toast, trying hard not to pay attention to the fact there was an obvious sex party between these guys last night and Maverick had to leave it for me. Like I can feel any more embarrassed than I already do. "Give it a rest, will yah," snaps Maverick. "We don't need a rundown of your night."

"Hey, don't be hating on me cos you missed out. But I still did right by you, brother—"

"Pres," Maverick growls more impatiently this time.

"They wanna stick around the club. I told them the rules and they're happy to help out around here." Maverick narrows his eyes. He doesn't look happy about this news. "What?" asks Grim innocently. "I thought you wanted some new pussy around here."

"First of all, it's too early for this bullshit," snaps Maverick. "Second of all, we can't take any new women right now. We're trying to make money, and you bring in two new mouths to feed?" I wince at Maverick's words. Is that how he feels about me and Ella? Not that I'm eating much, but still, it's two more bodies around here if he's struggling financially.

"You want the men to work hard, they need inspiration. Besides, Skye has her eyes fixed on you, man. You lucky son of bitch."

Maverick glances my way before dropping his fork down on his plate. It clatters and everyone turns to see what the drama is. "Nobody invites new people into this club without running it by me first. Is that clear?" he yells. A few of the guys nod, clearly confused as to why Maverick's in a mood. "This is not a free-for-all. We take people who can pay their way!" He stomps from the room, slamming the door behind him.

"What crawled up his ass?" mutters Grim, and I shrug. All I know is, I'm not paying my way and that has to change.

"Grim, how do I get a job?" I ask nervously.

"What you good at?" he asks, tucking into his breakfast.

I pretend to think over his question. Truth is, I dropped out of college after starting my A-levels, and I've never really had a job. I once worked in a supermarket, but it caused way too many arguments with Grant, so I gave it up. I shrug. "I can turn my hand to most things," I say, trying to put a positive spin on my lack of skills.

Grim smirks. "Don't say shit like that, or Pres will have you joining the club whores."

"Oh," I blush, "not that."

Grim laughs. "I was kidding. Leave it with me and I'll find you something."

I avoid Maverick for the rest of the day. His words keep playing on my mind, and I'm desperate to pay my way. It's not until dinnertime when I leave my bedroom and head into the kitchen, where I find Velvet looking through cupboards. "Do you want a hand?" I ask. She nods, and I join her. "Do you always cook for everyone?"

She shakes her head. "No. Everyone mucks in, but I drew the short straw tonight. I hate cooking," she mutters.

"I love cooking. I can take over if you want a break?"

"I was just gonna throw some sausages and mash on," she says, and I bite my lower lip.

"I make an amazing chicken curry," I say.

"I don't think we have the stuff for something fancy."

"I could nip out and get the ingredients. Is there a supermarket nearby?"

"Are you allowed out by yourself?" she asks. I shrug just as Meli walks in. "Meli, is she allowed out to the shop?"

"What for?"

"Food supplies," I say, and Meli nods.

"I'll take you. There's a money jar there," she adds, pointing to the glass jar. "Grab some, it's for food shopping."

I never did the food shopping. Grant took care of it, so I have no idea how much we'll need. I take a handful of screwed-up notes and follow Meli out the club to her car.

CHAPTER SEVEN

MAVERICK

"How was last night's collections?" I ask Crow.

"All good. Arthur gave me the cash, and I gave it to the treasurer."

I look at Lock, who confirms it with a nod. "Are the books looking slightly healthier?" I ask, and he nods again. "Great. Arthur has some more work on today, if Crow and Scar could pick that up. Ghost, I need you to shadow someone. Rylee's ex, the cop. I need evidence of his affair with his work partner. Just pictures and shit."

"No problems, Pres."

"Any more business?" I ask.

"Rylee asked me for work today," says Grim, and I frown. Why is she asking him instead of me? "I know we spoke about helping her to be independent and I suggested she become a club girl." He smirks, and I dive up. He holds his hands up, laughing. "Relax, I was kidding. She turned me down anyway."

I look around the room, finding everyone's eyes on me, and I release a breath. "I'll sort it," I mutter before storming from the room.

The smell of fresh spices hits my nostrils and I head for the kitchen. The only smell we usually get around here is greasy food, so I'm surprised when I see Rylee behind the counter, stirring a large pan on the oven. She glances up and smiles shyly. "I hope you like chicken curry."

"Bandia, that smells fucking amazing." I move closer and peer into the pan of thick, creamy sauce. "You didn't mention you can cook."

"Well, I don't want to give all my secrets away," she says, her cheeks flushing.

"It'll make a change to have something decent on the menu. I swear, if I smell one more sausage, I'll kill someone."

"I love cooking," she admits as she scoops some sauce onto a spoon and offers it to me. I take it willingly and close my eyes as the spice mixture hits my taste buds and they come alive. "Wow, that tastes even better than it smells." She glows under my praise, and it warms my fucking heart. "I didn't know we had this sort of stuff in the cupboards."

"Oh, you didn't. I had to go to the supermarket, but it didn't cost a lot. I tried to keep the price right down by using lower budget—" She stops abruptly when she realises I'm pissed.

"You went where?" I hiss, and she looks panicked.

Meli saunters in, freezing and staring back and forth between us before rushing around the counter to Rylee's side. "Jesus, Mav, don't be a dick. You're scaring her! It's okay, Rylee. Breathe."

"Who took Rylee out the club?" I demand.

"I did," she hisses. "We went in the car and were back within half an hour."

I pinch the bridge of my nose. "She can't be seen out with any of us just yet. It's too risky when we aren't ready to fight that arsehole. What the fuck were you thinking?" I yell. Rylee jumps in fright with each of my words, but I'm not mad at her. Meli knows better, and I won't have her use Rylee in her bid for more freedom.

Meli gives me the middle finger and turns her back to me. "Ignore him. He's a prick."

"You put her in danger!" I shout.

"I'm sorry. It was my idea," Rylee cuts in. "I wanted to help out around here, sort of pay my way until I get a job."

I close my eyes and try to regain control of my anger. I hate that she looks scared of me. "Meli knows better. This isn't on you."

"She doesn't need to hide," Meli yells. "You're keeping her prisoner just like he did!"

I feel the blood vessels in my forehead pumping, I'm so mad. "You are way outta line, Amelia. Go to your room."

"I'm not a fucking child, Mav. Stop treating me like one!" Grim rushes in, looking alarmed, and Meli groans. "Great, prison warden number two."

"Where were you today?" I growl, turning my anger on him.

"Busy, why? What's happened?" asks Grim.

"He was busy fucking the new whores." Meli smirks, and Grim narrows his eyes on her in warning.

"Because you were supposed to be watching her. Who was supposed to man the gates?"

"I dunno, I lost track. Rat, I think. What the hell did she do now?"

"She took Rylee to the supermarket unescorted," I hiss.

Grim groans. "Aw, shit, Meli. When are you gonna grow up?"

"I'm sick of this," snaps Meli as she marches out of the room. Rylee stands awkwardly for a second, looking like she wants to cry, and then she rushes out too.

"I thought she could be trusted, brother," Grim offers feebly.

"I'm sick of hearing fucking excuses. You will call me 'President' and you will stick to Meli like fucking glue. Now, find me the dickhead who was supposed to be manning the gates today!" I yell.

"Yes, Pres!" Grim spits the words like venom before storming out.

I laugh angrily. This place is a shitshow, and some days, I feel like I'm fighting a losing battle. I head to my office—I need a fucking drink.

Copper knocks on my office door. "What?" I snap.

"Something I said?" he asks, grinning. I signal for him to come in, and he closes the door. "Why'd yah look so stressed?"

"I don't think I'm cut out for this crap," I mutter, topping up my glass.

"Horse shit." Copper laughs, taking a seat. I pour a large vodka and slide it over to him. "Is it that brunette that's got you in a spin?"

I frown. "No," I say a little too quickly, and he laughs again, shaking his head.

"Eagle would rip into us whenever he was pissed with Brea. I used to think her Irish temper scared the shit outta him, so he'd take it out on us. He could fight us."

I scoff. "I seem to remember him fighting her all the goddamn time."

"That was later in their marriage. He couldn't move past Crow and Viper. But in the early days, when she was running rings around him," he smirks at the memory, "boy, she was a firecracker back then. Meli reminds me of her, defiant and feisty."

"She took Rylee out today. What if that bastard had seen them?"

"But he didn't."

"I hate to think what would have happened, Copper. She's still so weak, and he could force her back if he gets to speak with her alone like that."

"She's safe here. But you keep screaming like that and she might take off. She needs patience and understanding. A bit like a delicate baby bird."

"How can I protect her when I can't trust the people around me to stick to the rules?"

"You really do like her," he observes with a smirk.

I pause. "She ain't looking for that type of thing, so there's no way I can go there, but yeah, deep down, there's something that intrigues me about her in a way no other woman's interested me before." I shrug. I didn't even know I felt that till now. "I walked in on her last night. It was a real personal moment, and she clung to me, brother. It felt good. I wanna protect her and keep her safe. I don't even fucking know her properly yet, but something inside me is pulling me towards her and I can't stop it."

"Maybe take a step back, Pres. Like you said, she isn't looking for anything after the shit she's been through. We need you to have your head in the game. Put someone on Rylee to stop it happening again. If something's gonna happen between you two, it'll happen no matter how much space you put between you. If it's meant to be, it'll be."

"I don't trust anyone else with her."

"You trust Grim. Let him watch her and put Ripper on Meli. He used to watch over her when she was younger, and she never pisses him about. This is only until we get to the bottom of your dad's death."

I nod, because the old guy is right—I need to concentrate on the club. This shit I'm feeling is probably just pity. It'll pass.

RYLEE

Hadley pops her head into my room. "Come and eat. You cooked an amazing dinner, so you should join us."

I'm not feeling hungry, but Ella is, and she looks at me with hope, so I nod, and we head down. The dining room is the fullest I've ever seen. Brea is serving up when she spots me. "Damn, Rylee, this is amazing. The guys can't get enough." She hands me a bowl for Ella, but I decline the one she holds out for me.

Maverick's at the head of the table as usual, but this time, to his left, in the spot which is usually empty apart from when he made me sit there, is Skye. My step falters, not because she's there but because he has his hand on her knee possessively. I don't even know why that bothers me as much as it does.

The only space with two chairs free is right next to Skye. I lift Ella onto the next chair, and Skye smiles awkwardly. She's clearly not a kid person. Maverick doesn't even look up from his plate. "Aren't you hungry?" asks Meli. I shake my head, pouring myself a glass of water from the jug in the centre of the table. I notice Grim looking moody and wonder if he and Maverick had words after I left.

"Can we all just say a quick thank you to Rylee for this amazing dinner tonight," says Brea, joining the table. "It's been a long time since we had good home-cooked food like this." There's a rumbling of thanks and I smile shyly, hating all the attention. "Where did you learn to cook like this?" she asks.

"I taught myself." Grant would expect a full cooked meal every day, and there was never an acceptable excuse, even illness. The day I came home from the hospital with Ella, he made me stand in the kitchen and cook a roast dinner. I cried because I was so exhausted, so he punished me by making me stand in the garden in the rain, watching him eat through the window while my new baby cried for me. I shake my head to clear away the memory and catch Maverick staring at me. I smile, and he looks away.

One of the men whispers something to Meli. I feel her stiffen and then she turns to Maverick. "No," she says loudly, and he rolls his eyes. "I'll behave. I promise."

"Don't make a big deal," says Maverick, sighing.

"Why can't Grim watch me?"

"Because Grim is doing something else. Just for once, do as you're told, Meli. Your tantrums are boring me."

She falls silent, pushing her food around on her plate, which is weird, seeing as Meli usually has the last word. I make a note to ask her about that. She clearly hates the guy beside her, and he looks smug after her outburst.

After dinner, Maverick stands. "Rylee, my office, please," he says formally. Meli offers to watch Ella, so I follow him. He closes the door and takes a seat while I remain standing by the door. After his mood earlier, I don't know how to take him.

"You wanted a job," he begins, and I nod. "How about cooking for the guys here?"

I gasp. "You want me to cook?"

"Breakfast, Monday to Friday, and evening meal. The guys can grab their own lunch. If you make a list of things you'll need, I'll have that collected for you."

"That's great, thank you," I say.

"We'll pay you, of course," he adds.

"If you can't afford it," I begin, but he narrows his eyes, so I clamp my lips shut. I don't want to offend him, but I also don't wanna charge him if he has no money. Just letting me stay is payment enough.

"Who said I can't afford it?"

"Just you mentioned something earlier about having to feed people and I assumed—"

"You assumed wrong. I'll pay you a wage minus board and lodgings."

"Thanks. I appreciate it."

"If you need to go out, which I don't advise just yet, you're free to go whenever you please. All I ask is you have Grim with you. He'll be watching over you until the dust settles with your ex."

"I don't want to be any trouble," I mutter.

"That'll be all," he says, turning to his mobile.

I stand for a second, unsure why he's suddenly being so off with me. Apart from me going out earlier, I don't know what else I did wrong. "Maverick, I'm sorry if I've annoyed you today. It wasn't intentional." He looks up as I leave, and I just catch his sad expression as I close the door.

CHAPTER EIGHT

MAVERICK

It's been six weeks. Six weeks since Rylee and Ella came into my life, and fuck if I can't get her out my mind. I can't even fuck Skye because of the obsessive thoughts I have daily about Rylee. She stands in my kitchen cooking food for the guys, and I just wanna keep her to myself. I tried taking Copper's advice and staying away, but that shit don't apply when she's in my head.

I bang the gavel on the table to get the men's attention. We're making slow improvements to the club, and just lately, I've seen a real change in the mood of my brothers. Banter is high and I'm starting to build trust amongst them. Work is rolling in from the Taylors, and Arthur now uses my guys as security in his clubs. We're building up the bank balance and that makes us all relax a little.

"I need updates. Ghost, you wanna start?" He's spent three weeks watching Grant Carter. Leaning across the table, he lays some photographs out in the centre. They bring a smile to my face.

"Damn, how the fuck did you get so close?" asks Grim. "Looks like a porn shoot."

"They are *not* careful about where they're fucking."

"Remind me to close the blinds whenever you're around, you stealthy bastard," I say, grinning. These are exactly what we need to show Carter was having an affair behind Rylee's back.

"That's not the best bit." Ghost lays some more photographs showing Carter's lover leaving a private clinic. "He doesn't know it, but he's about to become a daddy all over again."

"Well, shit." I don't know how Rylee will take the news, but I get a small buzz knowing I'll have to go and speak with her. I'm always looking for an excuse these days. Since distancing myself from her, things have been awkward.

"He hasn't given up," adds Ghost. "He's paying a private agent to look for Rylee. Have you talked to her about what happens next?"

"Not yet. Now we have evidence, she can use this in her case to divorce him. We also have pictures of her bruising from the last time. Hadley wants to push him to sign the papers and use those pictures to persuade him. If he refuses, we'll threaten to press charges."

"H-how does Rylee f-f-feel about th-that?" asks Scar, and we all stare in his direction. He's still got his hood up—I don't know the last time I saw him without it—and we're all shocked he's spoken.

"I'll find out after we're done here," I say, exchanging a shocked look with Grim.

"Don't go upsetting her, Pres, cos we like her cooking," says Copper, and a few of the guys laugh. The best thing I did was hire her to cook—the menu's never been so healthy, and these guys love their food.

I head for the kitchen, where I usually find Rylee these days. I pause when I find Crow is talking to her. He's leaning across the counter, and she's smiling. Nothing Crow says is funny, so what the hell is she smiling about? He looks back over his shoulder and rolls his eyes. "Can I have a word?" I snap, and she begins chopping something green. She thinks I'm talking to Crow. "Rylee," I say, and she looks up, almost dropping the knife.

"Sorry, I thought you meant Crow. Of course." She blushes, and I feel like an arse for snapping. Instead of apologising like I should, I head for the office. She follows, wiping her hands down her jeans. I got Meli to take her shopping, under Grim's watchful eye, of course, and she got a whole new wardrobe. She's looking healthier too. The dark circles under her eyes are gone, just like the bruises. She doesn't wince in pain with every move anymore and she's not as skittish as she was when she first arrived.

"I thought you'd like to look at some of these," I say, throwing a couple of brochures on the desk. She takes one and looks it over. "I don't know how you feel about Ella starting school, but the new term is fast approaching, according to my mum."

"Thanks, I'll take a look."

"I also wanted to talk to you about Grant. Maybe you should take a seat." She does, but her whole demeanour has changed. She sits stiffly and her face is rigid, void of any emotion. "He's been out of your life for weeks," I say. "We need to think about making that more permanent."

"Do you think he's still looking for me?"

"Yes," I say bluntly, and she chews on her bottom lip. "I've had him followed, Rylee." I give her a minute to process that before placing a few of the less offensive pictures on the desk. "We needed evidence of him cheating. Along with some CCTV I have from the Fun Day, we also have these."

"Right." She nods for far too long, staring at the images.

"There's something else." She leans back in the chair, gripping the wooden arms. "She's pregnant." Her face remains blank. "Did you hear me?" This time, she nods. "Ghost seems to think Grant doesn't know about it."

"He'll be over the moon, I'm sure. He wanted another baby."

"I think he wanted another baby with you to keep you where he wanted you. I'm not convinced he'll be happy about this. Why would he be looking for you if he was happy with her?"

"Because he hates to lose. He decides everything, and he didn't decide to let me go."

"Which brings me to my next thing. The divorce."

She sucks in a breath. "I can't afford a solicitor to sort all that."

"We have it covered. The firm Hadley works for does work for the club. They can draw up the papers and have them served on Grant as soon as you agree."

She looks worried. "Okay."

"But the only snag is, he'll know where you are."

Panic crosses Rylee's face, and she shakes her head. "No, I'm not ready for that."

I crouch down in front of her, taking both her hands in my own. It's the first time I've been this close to her since I spent the night with her in my arms. "Rylee, listen to me. I've kept you safe this long, and I'll keep you safe for as long as you need it. He can't take you against your will. We have evidence that shows he's cheating, so if he's got any sense, he'll agree to the divorce without a fuss. If he doesn't, we'll fight him every step."

"That will cost money," she cries out.

"I'll worry about that. You keep cooking amazing meals and let me worry about the rest."

She stands abruptly, taking me by surprise. "No. I can't let you keep rescuing me. I have to sort myself out. You've done so much for me already." She rushes from the office, leaving me confused.

RYLEE

It was too much. Having him so close, filling my nose with his stupid manly smell, and then touching me with his oversized hands. I grip the wall and take some deep breaths. Maverick's been avoiding me for weeks, since he treated me so coldly in his office. I don't know how he makes me think things I shouldn't just by touching me. I've never had a man make me feel like he does, and it's pathetic. He pays me a smidgen of attention, and I panic and run out of there. I roll my eyes. He must think I'm crazy.

"What did Pres want?" I spin round, pressing my back to the wall. Skye eyes me with contempt. I've seen her behave like this to all the women Maverick speaks to.

"It was about my ex," I mumble. I don't want confrontation with Skye. She's got the whole mean girl thing going on, and I have bigger things to worry about.

"Don't you feel bad?" she asks, lighting up a cigarette.

"About?"

"Sponging off the club. I have to fuck to earn my keep, and you cook a few dinners."

"Fucking isn't really my thing," I mutter, shrugging. "Not got a lot of experience."

"Yeah, I can't imagine Maverick fucking you. He likes his women a little crazy." She leans against the wall. "The things that man can do," she adds, grinning. "And him and Grim together," she giggles, "let's just say I have trouble walking the next day."

"Are you seeing him?" I ask, cringing the second the words leave my mouth.

She laughs. "Sweetheart, girls like me don't get the guy. Until a woman is claimed around here, she's anyone's. You should be careful—I've seen the way Crow looks at you. Maybe he's thinking of making you his whore."

"I just do the cooking," I say feebly.

"Around here, you do what they say or you're out, simple as that."

"But Hadley and Meli—"

"Are Mav's sisters. No one can touch them. They're the sort of girls who get married before sex. Mav would need to approve any boyfriends." She pushes off the wall, flicking her cigarette to the ground and crushing it under her heel. "Don't get me wrong, I like being Mav's fuck piece. It's better than some of the alternatives. But we're just the hired help, so don't get comfortable, unless you wanna end up like me." She walks with a sway, and I worry my bottom lip. I can't have sex with Crow. Maverick said I just had to cook, but what if he changes his mind and I end up trapped here too?

I head back inside to continue with dinner. Maybe once I'm divorced, I can offer weekly repayments to cover the costs and then find a place to live of my own. I smile at the thought of me and Ella having our own place. It's never been a possibility before, but after three weeks, I've already made eight hundred pounds. Mav told me he takes the rent off before he pays me and he won't accept more.

As I pass his office, I hear cries of ecstasy. She really is his own private call girl. And for the first time since arriving, I feel a stab of jealousy, because if I have to screw anyone around here, I'd choose him every time. What kind of woman does that make me?"

It's a few days later when I sign the divorce papers. It feels like a weight has been lifted even though I know this isn't going to be easy, but it's another step closer to freedom. In the beginning, I was happy to hide away here in the safety of the club, but now I've been away from Grant for a few weeks, I'm longing to spread my wings a little and go further. So, when I knock on Maverick's office door, it's in the hope he'll take me out. I feel safer with him over anyone else.

"What?" he barks, and I hesitate before stepping in.

"I looked over the brochures for schools," I say. "I was wondering if I could go and look at them. I know you need an appointment, but I just wanna look from the outside and get a feel for the places."

He nods. "I'll get Grim to take you. He's busy today, so I'll let you know when it'll be." He goes back to staring at his laptop screen. Disappointed, I retreat, since he's clearly busy.

Hadley's out in the yard with Ella. I sit down on the grass beside her and watch my daughter enjoying the freedom of the backyard. Back home, we weren't allowed in the garden unless Grant was there, and even then, it wasn't for long. "The papers are being delivered today," Hadley informs me, and I nod. I know the news won't go down well with Grant, and I'm apprehensive about what he'll do once he knows where I am. "Maverick got a couple of the guys to go along with the solicitor. I think he thought there might be trouble."

"Grant isn't stupid. He'll come up with something creative once he's thought about it." I pause for a minute, then ask, "Do you get fed up with club life like Meli does?"

She shrugs. "I don't know any difference. Meli wasn't always like this. She wanted to marry a biker, become an ol' lady. We used to plan our weddings together."

"Oh, I imagined she'd always been like this."

"She changed overnight. We stopped talking properly." She pauses before adding, "I don't know why I'm telling you this."

"What was Maverick like as a kid?" I ask.

She smiles. "Bossy. He thought he was the shit because of who he was. Dad always made it clear he'd be the Pres one day, and he took it seriously."

"I bet you miss your dad."

"Sometimes," she says vaguely. "Do you like it here?"

I nod. "I'm so grateful to everyone. I'd still be trapped in that life or maybe worse if Nelly hadn't called for help that day. Sometimes, one decision can change your whole life. I can't wait for the day when I can walk down the street and not have to look over my shoulder."

"I hope that happens for you soon, Rylee. Have you thought about what you want to do after? Once it's all sorted?"

I shrug. Thinking about leaving here makes me sad. "I've never been on my own before. I've always had Grant, for as long as I remember. Certainly, for my adult life so far. It's scary to think about being on my own."

"Well, you'll always have a place here."

I smile. "Don't you have to be family to earn a place here? Or be a club whore?"

She laughs. "No, who told you that?"

"Skye. She said I'd have to earn my keep."

"Jesus, don't listen to the club girls, Rylee. She has her eye on Mav and will say anything to get rid of competition." She slaps her hand over her mouth. "I shouldn't have said that."

"Competition?" I repeat. "I'm hardly that."

"Are you joking? Rylee, you're stunning. I can't believe you've not been swept off your feet yet. I think the guys are trying to be respectful because of what you've been through, but I feel like once you've moved forward, there'll be no end to the proposals and dates."

I blush. "Please," I mumble bashfully.

"You pay your way by looking after the guys in the most important way—through their stomachs. You're ol' lady material, and they all know it."

"Skye said we're the hired help."

"Skye is a cow. She thinks fucking Grim is her ticket in here." Hadley sounds bitter.

"Yeah, she told me about him and Maverick."

"My brother hasn't touched the skank. No, that's all on Grim."

I don't mention I heard them in his office. "You like Grim?" I ask, and her face turns crimson. "Oh, sorry, I didn't mean to embarrass you."

"It doesn't matter anyway, he likes my sister so—"

"Meli?" I almost screech in disbelief. "They act like they hate each other."

"She hates him, but he loves her. He has for a long time." She sighs. "Forget I said anything. We should take Ella in. It's getting hot out here."

∞

In the clubhouse, Brea takes Ella from me. "Go and relax. I'll babysit tonight. As soon as the guys are back, I'm sure they'll tell you how it went, but right now, you need to take your mind off it." She's right. I've been a nervous wreck all day, and when I still hadn't heard by dinner, I ended up burning the rice and having to re-cook a whole panful.

Hadley hooks her arm with mine. "That offer is too good to turn down. We'll get a bottle of wine and go and watch the sunset." It sounds good enough. I like Hadley—she's like me, and I feel like we're connecting.

The bar is chaos. Nelly has invited a couple of her friends, and Meli has tagged on to the party vibe. They end up following us out, which is nice because I need the entertainment, but Hadley withdraws slightly. I keep my arm hooked with hers and make sure I stay with her when we find a spot to sit on the grass. Nelly introduces her friends as Ember and Gracie. They're our age, making Meli and Hadley the youngest, but you wouldn't tell, even with Meli's craziness as she necks vodka neat from the bottle.

We pass around the vodka and then share wine. It's chilled, and even when Skye joins us, it doesn't ruin my vibe. Eventually, Crow and Dice make it out. I ignore the fact that Crow chooses to sit right next to me while Skye gives a knowing smile.

CHAPTER NINE

MAVERICK

Scar and Ghost get back late. I sent them to work for Arthur for the evening right after delivering the divorce papers to Grant. They join me in the office, and I down a shot of vodka to calm myself. "Come on then, hit me with it."

"Pres, he was calm. Like really calm. It caught us off guard," explains Ghost.

"He didn't say anything?"

"Not really. He took them, and the solicitor explained Rylee's position and advised him to have his own solicitor look at the papers. He agreed, and we left."

"That's good then, right? Maybe he's moved on with his side piece and everyone can live happily ever after?"

Ghost shrugs. "Tell you what, though, I could get used to that kind of work. It's a good call helping these women. I felt good today, like we were making a difference." I smile, because it's the sort of thing I need to hear to keep the guys motivated.

"I'll go and tell Rylee the news. She's been a nervous wreck all afternoon, according to Mum."

"She was out in the yard with a few of the girls. Crow was looking a little cosy," says Ghost.

I head straight out, and he's right, my little brother looks very fucking cosy next to Rylee, like there isn't enough fucking space to spread out a bit. Skye spots me and makes a beeline, throwing her arms around my neck and pushing her tits against my chest. Skye's been throwing herself at me for weeks and it's getting boring. I asked Grim to distract her and get her off my back, but she isn't taking the hint. I quickly unwrap her from me. I have one goal tonight and that's to get Crow away from Rylee.

I crouch down in front of Rylee. She looks flustered and a little drunk. "The guys are back," I say, and I hold out my hand, which she takes. Crow narrows his eyes, and I smile, winking at him as I help her stand. I keep hold of her hand as we head away from the others towards the back of the club, where there's an open space leading into a small woodland. "They said he took it well."

"That's worse," she mutters, her eyes full of worry.

"Maybe, but for now, things are okay."

"I hope he's moved on," she whispers, her voice laced with desperation.

"We've got plenty to hit him with if he hasn't. Try not to worry." We step into the trees and stop when we're out of view from the others.

"I hate him so much. If he died tomorrow, I wouldn't shed a single tear. Does that make me bad?" She leans against a tree and blinks up at me with those blue eyes I can't help but get lost in. I rest a hand against the tree, above her head, caging her in.

"It makes you human. He's a monster."

"We should head back. Skye will get mad," she says, and I frown.

"Why would Skye get mad?"

"Well, cos you and her are . . ." she trails off, not wanting to say the word.

"Fucking?" I ask, and she nods. I laugh. "No, we're not. She and Grim are fucking."

"I heard you," she says, "in your office."

"That wasn't me, but thanks for the heads up. I'll kill that motherfucker. Jesus, I hope they didn't do it on my desk." She giggles and the sound lifts my heart. We fall silent, and I stare at her, lost in her innocent eyes. All I can think about is kissing her. I know I can't, or shouldn't, but fuck, I want to so badly. Her breathing is just as rapid as my own. Maybe she's thinking the same, but she's drunk and her judgment is out. Lifting on her tiptoes, I keep my eyes on hers, daring her to do it. Her tongue darts out, wetting her lips.

"Thank you for everything," she whispers, her eyes falling to my lips. She edges closer, and I watch her close her eyes just as her lips brush my own. She pauses, lingering for a second before pulling away. It's like a dream, and I feel like a kid again, smiling like a goofy teenager. Then, she moves to the side, escaping my cage. Throwing a smile back over her shoulder, she heads back out of the trees and towards the group. And I follow behind like the ball-less bitch I've become after one fucking lip brush. I shake my head and laugh. Grim would rip the piss if he saw that.

Grim hands me a beer and sits beside me. Half the damn club is sitting out here, but it's calm and just what I needed after the stress of today. "When are you gonna stop watching her?" he asks.

"Dunno what you're talking about." I smirk, taking a pull on my beer.

"Damn if she ain't doing that cute little smirk right back at you," he observes. "What the fuck is going on between you?"

"Nothing, brother. She's just happy that the bastard didn't kick off."

"And she's paying her gratitude back with flirty looks?"

"I haven't noticed," I lie. Truth is, I'm replaying that moment we shared over and over in my mind.

There's a low thud coming from somewhere. In my hazy sleep-fogged mind, it sounds distant, but the longer it continues, the more awake I become until I'm sitting up in bed and looking around. "Pres, get up." Grim bangs on my bedroom door, making me jump out of bed and pull it open. He's putting on some shorts as he pants, "Police raid," then rushes back along the hall to wake the other brothers.

My first thought is Rylee. She'll be scared. The club's used to this sort of shit, although we haven't seen it for a couple of years at least. I pull on some jeans, but by the time I reach the end of the hallway, torches are blinding me as the officers shine them in my face, and I'm being pushed back to my room. Two cops keep their hands on my shoulders while they listen to their radios. A crackly voice confirms they have the club locked down and everyone secure. Fuck, there must be a lot of cops in here. "What the fuck's this about?" I growl.

"All in good time, big man," one says, smirking.

"I need to check on someone," I snap.

"We'll move everyone downstairs shortly. You don't mind if we cuff you, do yah? Don't want you getting any silly ideas," he adds, pulling out the metal restraints. I roll my eyes as he slaps them around my wrists. I've learnt from experience there's no point in fighting them.

I'm led downstairs into the main room, where most of my brothers are already seated. There's an unusual silence amongst us. They caught us off guard, and because we don't run in criminal circles so much these days, we don't have an informant from the inside. I make a mental note to change that. Glancing around, I don't see Rylee. Grim seems to read my expression and he shrugs.

An important-looking man approaches. He's not in uniform, which means he's from the Crime Investigation Unit. Only those assholes wear cheap suits. "You in charge around here?" he asks, and I nod. "Then this is for you." He holds up a piece of paper. "This gives us the right to search the premises for drugs." I roll my eyes. "We had an anonymous tipoff."

"I don't give a shit. You won't find anything unless it's for personal use. There's someone missing," I say. "My," I pause because I almost said 'woman', "friend isn't down here." He looks around too. "Her ex is one of you lot. He's dangerous and a threat to her."

The man laughs. "Got proof of that, have you?"

"Please. I'll comply with all this shit, but someone needs to go check on her. Especially if you have Officer Carter here tonight." Something passes over his face, and he nods for a nearby cop to go and check. Finally, I sigh in relief.

RYLEE

The banging causes me to jump out of bed. At first, I thought it was one of the guys' headboards—that happens a lot—but when I realise it isn't, I run towards the connecting door to get Ella. I almost die on the spot. My baby girl is in the arms of that monster, and I have to pinch myself to make sure I'm not in a nightmare.

Ella is crying and reaching for me, but Grant holds her tightly against him. Gripping the door frame to stop my legs from buckling, terror rips through me.

"Hey, beautiful. Fancy seeing you here."

"How did you—"

"It was on the paperwork you had your thugs serve me today." That doesn't explain how he knew the room I was in. He moves towards me, and I back up, but he catches me by the hair and pulls my face to his. It contorts with rage. "You think I'm gonna let you divorce me? Take my daughter? To live here," he looks around and grins evilly, "with bikers?"

"Let me go," I hiss, trying to push him away. Ella screams louder.

"I'm gonna break you, Rylee," he threatens.

"You did that already," I cry out as his hold on my hair gets tighter.

"I'm gonna take my time. Ruin you slowly until you have nothing left. You think these arseholes will protect you forever when I start causing them trouble? You'll never be able to leave me until I say you can."

"I'll tell the police. I'll go to your boss and tell him," I cry out, and he laughs, placing Ella down. She tries to come to me, but he pulls me away and shoves me into my bedroom, slamming the connecting door. I hear her cries through the door, and it breaks my heart. I thought for one stupid second that it wouldn't happen again.

"I'll tell the police," he mimics in a stupid voice. "You take this any further and I'll kill Ella. You see how easy it is for me to get in here? I'll take everything and everyone until you have nothing. I'm not scared to go to prison so long as you're not walking this earth without me."

We hear footsteps approach, and Grant's face changes. He looks relaxed and calm as he pulls me hard into his chest and turns me away from the door. It opens, but I don't see who's there because he's pressing my face against him. "Boss wants to know what's taking so long?" asks a man.

"Sorry. Just catching up with my wife. We haven't seen each other since she left," says Grant, sounding heartbroken.

"Sorry, man, but she needs to be downstairs with the others. Is that a kid crying?"

"Yeah. Ella, she's next door, but I was comforting this one. Total emotional wreck," he says with a laugh. I hear the connecting door open and Ella rushes to me, wrapping her arms around my legs. Grant releases me and swoops her up. "Hey, baby girl, I've missed you." He rains kisses on her cheek, but she grabs me and pulls herself into my arms and away from him. He gives me a warning glare before turning to his colleague and smiling. "All done."

Downstairs, I keep my head lowered as we enter the room. I can feel eyes burning into me and the tension in the atmosphere could be cut with a knife. "What took so long?" barks a man in a suit.

"Sorry, boss, emotional reunion."

"Are you okay?" the man asks me, and I nod without a word.

"No, she's not fucking okay," yells Maverick.

"You'd have to be blind to think she was," adds Grim, "but then he's your own, so you're gonna protect him."

"As I've already said, if you have a complaint, go down the proper channels. This is a separate incident," says the man firmly.

"Rylee," snaps Maverick, and I hold Ella tighter. "Rylee," he repeats, "look at me." I raise my head and meet his eyes. Something about Maverick calms me. He'll know what to do. "Are you okay, Bandia?" I nod, feeling rage pulsating from Grant as he watches our exchange.

"Rylee, are you here against your will?" asks Grant, gripping my upper arm in what looks to everyone like a gentle move, when in actual fact, he's pinching me.

"No," I say firmly.

"Are you sure, because you look scared."

"She's scared of you, arsehole," yells Maverick.

"You do know my wife is vulnerable."

"Soon to be ex," says Grim.

"We'll see what her doctor says when I request a psychiatric assessment," Grant says calmly. I glare at him, and he smiles. "You can't take care of my daughter, sweetheart. You know you're not well. Have these guys seen you at your worst yet? The way you get without your meds?"

"You didn't give two shits about that when you left her alone in the house to look after Ella," snaps Mav.

His boss returns from speaking to some other officers. "Let's clear out," he orders. "Release these men from the handcuffs, there's nothing here."

"I told you there wouldn't be," says Maverick.

Grant runs a finger down my arm, moving uncomfortably close. "I'm gonna start with him," he whispers. "If you're a good girl, I'll let you watch."

Once they're gone, Maverick rushes over and wraps his arms around me and Ella. I burst into tears, sobbing as he gently shushes me and strokes my hair. "It's okay, Bandia. He's gone."

"He's never gonna go. He'll always come for me, and unless I go back, he'll keep doing stuff like this."

"So?" Maverick shrugs. "Apart from it interrupting our sleep, what's a little dawn raid gonna do?"

I pull away. Everyone's starting to head back off to bed. Brea takes Ella, and I'm surprised when Ella cuddles into her. She trusts her, and it makes me smile. "It'll soon wear thin. He's made threats to Ella, to you . . ."

He moves my hair behind my ear and smiles. "I'll take care of him. We're ready for this fight, remember?"

"We weren't ready for this," I snap. "He plays dirty and he's gonna win."

"I won't let him."

"You can't protect me forever, Maverick. You didn't ask for this drama. It's my mess and I have to face up to it."

"By giving up? By going back?" he says, stepping away from me. I miss his warmth immediately.

It would be the easy option, after all. He wanted to get in my head, so I'd do exactly that, but I'm stronger than that now. "No. By finally stepping up. I'm gonna fight him every step of the way. Let's start by discrediting him like Hadley said. I want his colleagues to know who they work with."

Maverick smiles, and I stand a little taller under his appraising gaze. "There's my Bandia, a true goddess." His hand grazes my cheek, but his thumb lingers a little longer, stroking back and forth. "You're perfect," he adds.

I stare at his lips, silently begging for them to taste my own. "If you wanna kiss me, you have to make the move," he whispers, and I gasp slightly. I've sobered up since earlier and I'm not feeling as confident, but I find myself tipping my head back slightly and moving closer. His other hand cups the back of my head, and as I press my lips to his, I feel like I'm floating. This time, instead of letting me pull away, his thumbs brush along my chin and he holds me in place, kissing me back.

It's soft, gentle, and so much more than I expected. He sweeps his tongue into my mouth and a groan escapes him. It's the hottest thing I've ever heard. When he pulls back, I want to cry out in frustration. He smiles, pressing his forehead to mine. "Fuck, baby, if that wasn't the hottest kiss I've ever had." I blush, and he groans again. "You're killing me here. Go to bed before I carry you into my office and bend you over my desk." I blush deeper. Something about that statement has me clenching my thighs together.

CHAPTER TEN

MAVERICK

"Bandia," says Grim, grinning like a Cheshire cat as he barges into my office, looking as fresh as a daisy.

"Why'd yah look so happy today? Thought the morning cop call would ruin your mood for the entire day," I say, leaning back in my chair.

"My boy is all grown up. He's calling a woman 'goddess', which means he's falling head over heels," he says.

"Grow up."

"Are you denying your feelings for a certain brunette?" he asks.

"I'm saying it's none of your business."

"I get it," he says, grinning. "She's a great cook, she's cute and innocent looking—"

"Shut the fuck up," I snap.

"I'd definitely fu—" I dive up from my chair, and he laughs, falling back onto the couch and holding his hands up defensively. "Kidding," he gasps. I relax, taking my seat again. "I take it we're not sharing this one," he adds, breaking into another fit of laughter.

"Maybe you should think of doing the same."

"What? Finding a goddess?" he scoffs. "Fuck no. I'm having way too much fun being VP and having pussy on tap."

"I'm serious. This club needs stability. We need ol' ladies to complete this place."

Grim shakes his head, groaning dramatically. "Next, you'll say you want kids running around." When I don't laugh, he sits up straighter. "Shit, you do! What's this voodoo magic she's cast on you?"

"I don't mean me, dickhead. But this club needs that family vibe. Who will continue it after we're gone? It'll die with us. Without family, it's basically a frat club!"

"There ain't nothing wrong with a fraternity club, brother."

"Apart from we're an MC club."

"We got church, we don't have time to discuss marriage and babies." Grim stands. "I feel like you've aged me in that conversation. Put your crazy idea to the brothers, they'll shit themselves."

I follow him into church. I don't know where that conversation came from. I've gone from kissing Rylee to talking about ol' ladies and settling down. She's not ready for that sort of commitment, but it gets me hard just thinking about making her mine.

"How the fuck do we stop that happening again?" asks Copper. "That shit's just gonna keep piling on the pressure."

"And he sure as fuck ain't gonna sign no divorce papers," adds Lock.

"What will happen if he's paid the doc off to give a bad psych report? He'll have her sectioned," says Tatts.

I smile. These guys are showing they care. My plan to bring the guys together seems to be working. "We can't give up. I never said fighting for these women would be easy. We just have to work out how to play the game. Not every rescue will involve a cop. He's got an unfair advantage on us."

"Dice called me ten minutes ago to say he'd been stopped for a search. They've got markers on our back, Pres." Dice huffs.

"I've got Rylee an appointment with a good doctor who works for Arthur Taylor. We'll get as many psych reports as we need to prove Rylee is sane. We just have to stay one step ahead. I'm working on getting an insider to give us the heads up."

"And who's paying for all this?" asks Crow.

"The club," I reply, daring him to question me further.

"That's got to be costing us a pretty penny," he mutters.

"You got a problem with that?"

"Thought you'd wanna help Rylee, brother, seeing as you've been trying to get her in your bed for weeks," says Grim.

"I was hoping the Pres would make her a club whore," retorts Crow.

"She pays her way," I growl.

"In your bed?" he snaps.

"You're fucking out of line," I yell, moving to him. A few brothers step in my way, and Crow smirks.

"Look at you getting all bent out of shape over this bitch. You saw I liked her and you've swooped in!" he shouts.

"Get him out of here," orders Grim, and some of the guys drag him away.

"If anyone has a problem with the club paying to help vulnerable women escape abusive fuckers just like Carter, then come see me. We'll talk about it." I slam the gavel on the table and storm out. I need to have it out with that smug prick, but right now, I need to get Rylee to her appointment.

I sit in the car outside the doctor's office. We couldn't bring the bike because I didn't wanna risk getting pulled over by the cops and missing this appointment. Rylee grips the door handle. "Is everything okay?" she asks, and I feel like a dick. I've been silent the entire journey, my mind focussed on Crow and his outburst.

"Yeah, just shit on my mind."

"Anything I can help with?"

I laugh at her attempt to help me when she's got so many of her own problems. "Nah, I'll be alright. Go and see this doc, then I'll take you to lunch."

"In a restaurant?" she asks, her eyes dancing with excitement.

I shrug. "Sure. Whatever you want."

Rylee's gone for forty minutes. When she returns, she looks happier. "He's gonna write it all out and send it to me."

"He didn't section you then?" I joke, pulling out into traffic.

"He seems to think I'm completely normal. He confirmed I'm thinking very clearly."

"Good. Now, let's go eat, I'm starving."

I indicate to turn into the car park of a Mexican restaurant, and as I pull in, I see the car behind speed up. It catches the right side, sending our car spinning into oncoming traffic. As we come to a stop, I hear tyres screeching to try and avoid hitting us. Rylee's screams die down, and I turn to her, gripping her pale face in my hands. "Are you okay?" I ask. She nods, her eyes wide with shock. I look around and find cars are stopped all around us. How the fuck they managed to avoid us is a miracle. The car that hit us is long gone. I get out to assess the damage, and another car driver joins me as I stare at the dented back end.

"Shit. That was a straight hit and run," he says, gasping. "I didn't have time to get the registration plate."

"Don't worry," I say. "I have a garage that can repair the damage. Thanks, though."

I get back in the car and sigh in relief when it starts. Driving into the restaurant car park, I put a call in to Trucker to request the recovery truck. I don't wanna risk driving us in case that little hit and run wasn't a coincidence.

"Trucker's gonna be ten minutes. Shall we grab some food?" I suggest.

Rylee shakes her head. "I'm not hungry. Let's go back to the club."

I sigh. I can see her withdrawing and I hate he's got this power over her.

RYLEE

I go straight to my room when we get back to the club. Mav needs to sort out the car, and I feel exhausted with all the worry and stress wondering what Grant will do next. I'm not stupid—it was no coincidence we were ran off the road today.

It's mid-afternoon when Mav knocks on my door. "You must be hungry now," he says, and I shrug. I guess I am hungry, but I can't think of food right now. He doesn't ask anything else. Instead, he takes my hand and leads me towards his room. We go straight out onto the balcony, where there's a table set with afternoon tea. I smile. Afternoon tea isn't something a biker thinks about, and this has Hadley written all over this.

"Hadley helped," he says, grinning.

I laugh. "I didn't imagine you making sandwiches."

"I just wanted to see that smile," he says. His eyes darken and he stares at my lips. I know it's coming as he moves towards me with the stealth of a tiger. He cages me against the railings and closes his mouth over mine in another toe-curling kiss. "I've been wanting to do that all morning," he mutters.

I run my fingers through his hair, pulling him back for another. He's addictive, and after the day we've had, I'm grabbing the chance while I can. I push my body as close as I can get it and wrap my arms around his neck. The kiss turns hungry, and this time, it's me who lets a groan escape. Maverick pulls away, panting. "Shit, give me a minute," he hisses, stepping back and hanging his head. My eyes fall to the bulge in his jeans, and I blush. The fact I did that to him makes me feel powerful, a sensation I haven't felt in years. I throw myself at him, taking him by surprise. He stumbles back a few steps, catching me, and when I wrap my legs around his waist, he slams me against the wall. Kissing me, he moves his mouth down to my neck and along my jaw. "What do you want, Rylee?"

I pause, looking into his hungry eyes, my breaths coming fast and uneven. "You."

"I don't want to rush you on this," he mutters.

"I want you to show me what it's like," I whisper. He stares back, confused. "To want it and not be forced." He's taken aback by my confession, and I panic, not wanting to ruin the mood. "I want to choose when I do it, and I'm choosing now . . . with you."

He nods, still looking unsure, and carries me into his room, carefully laying me on the bed. He braces himself over me, staring down at me with a serious expression. "You wanna stop at any point, just say the word and I'll stop." I nod, and he kneels between my legs and pulls his shirt over his head, dropping it to the floor. I take in his strong, toned chest and let my eyes roam over his tattoos. He unfastens his belt, and my eyes fall there, eager to feel his strong body back over me. Shoving his jeans below his backside, he falls back over me, kissing me gently. I miss the hunger from moments ago, replaced with gentle kisses along my shoulder.

Closing my eyes, I enjoy the feel of Maverick's hands running up my waist and disappearing under my top. He massages circles over my ribs until his thumbs brush the underside of my breasts. He finds the centre, front clasp to my bra, unclipping it. His hands work their way to my breasts, gently massaging them and occasionally flicking his thumb over my sensitive nipples. I pull my top over my head and drop it to the floor. He stares down at my breasts before lowering his head and sucking a nipple into his warm mouth. My back arches off the bed as a warm sensation rushes through my body.

Maverick takes his time to tease me with his tongue, occasionally smiling each time I react with a shudder or a moan. He backs up, sliding down until his face is between my legs, and I throw my arm over my eyes to hide my embarrassment. I've never had a man down there like that, and as he slides my leggings and panties down, I resist the urge to bat him away. He kisses my inner thigh, nipping the skin and working his way up.

When I feel his hot breath against my own heat, I automatically try to close my legs. He sniggers, using his hands to spread them open again and hold them in place. His tongue darts out, catching my throbbing bud, and I cry out in surprise. He places his arms under my thighs, wrapping them around to hold my hands. He presses his tongue there again, and this time when I jerk, he's holding me in place. He runs his tongue along my opening and hums his approval. I'm too turned on to be embarrassed as he continues to lick and taste me. When he sucks my clitoris into his mouth, I cry out again, thrashing my head from side to side as his onslaught continues.

I'm writhing around on the bed, not sure if I need to move closer or pull away, and then a powerful sensation tears through me. I squeeze Maverick's hands in mine and pant through the explosions shuddering through me. When they slow to no more than a tingle, he finally pulls away, and I lay lifeless, trying to catch my breath. He fumbles around with a condom packet. "That was the most amazing thing I've ever watched," he murmurs, crawling up my body and settling between my legs. "Now, I need you to do it again," he lines his erection at my entrance, "on my cock."

Easing inside me, he lets me adjust to his size with each push. I feel every inch, and when he eventually stops, he smiles down at me and whispers, "Relax." His lips move against mine, and I begin to. He places his hands either side of my head and withdraws before repeating the slow movement. "You okay?" he asks.

I want to laugh and tell him I'm better than okay. This is the greatest I've felt in a long time, maybe ever, but I nod, too turned on to find the right words. "You know how sexy you look right now, all flustered and aroused?" he pants out. Closing his eyes for a second, he pauses, then drops down closer, burying his head in the crook of my neck and groaning. "Fuck, I need to come so badly."

He waits, trying to gain some control. "We need to change position or I'm done." He grins, pulling from me. "What position do you like?" he asks, and I feel my face burn. The only position I know is one where Grant pins me down and hurts me. Maverick seems to read my mind and moves in for another kiss, distracting me from my thoughts. Guiding my leg over him until I'm straddling him, he smiles, resting his head back against the headboard. "I wanna see you." I watch him nervously. I've never ridden a guy before, but he doesn't give me much time to think about it before he's pushing back inside me. I grip his shoulders, and he clasps onto my hips with his hands, showing me how to move. I get into a rhythm pretty quickly, finding one I like.

Maverick's eyes are hooded as he watches me grind against him. He leans forward and flicks his tongue over my nipple, and I jerk, setting off that chain reaction again. But this time, I'm in control and I chase the feeling, slamming hard up and down. His hand moves between us, finding my swollen bud and rubbing it until I'm crying out in ecstasy. He grabs me by the hips and begins thrusting up into me, chasing his own orgasm. He comes on a roar, and it's hotter than the growl he emits when he kisses me.

I stare in wonderment as the muscles in his neck strain, then I lean forward and run kisses there. He releases a low groan and finally stills. I bury my face against his neck as he wraps his arms around me. We're slick with sweat and our mixed juices, but I'm in no hurry to move away from this glorious man.

CHAPTER ELEVEN

MAVERICK

"She looks so happy," says Mum, nudging her shoulder against my own. We're watching Rylee spin Ella around, then they tumble onto the grass, giggling. "Does that have anything to do with you?"

"Maybe," I say, "or maybe she's just happy to be safe."

"You're a good boy, Kilian. You always have been."

Rylee joins us, and Mum swaps, chasing after Ella. She lies beside me, and I turn onto my side. "All I can think about," I whisper in her ear, "is being inside of you." I kiss her, but she freezes, so I pull back, frowning. "What?"

She sits up, looking around anxiously. "I just wasn't expecting you to... yah know... out here."

I look around too. Everyone's having their own conversations. "Does it matter if people see?" She shrugs, but I can tell by her expression it bothers her. "Rylee, talk to me. How will I know what you want if you don't tell me?"

"I don't wanna upset anyone," she utters.

I narrow my eyes. "You mean Crow?" I snap.

Her eyes widen and she shakes her head. "No, why would Crow be upset? I meant the women."

"I'm pretty sure Hads and Meli don't give a crap."

"The other women," she says through gritted teeth as Lady, one of the club whores, and Skye pass us.

"Hey, Pres," says Skye, pouting her lips and sticking out her chest.

Ignoring her, I grin. "Oh, you mean the whores."

"I hate you calling them that," she mutters. "Skye already hates me. I don't wanna give her an actual reason." I climb over Rylee's body and push her to lie back down. "Mav, please," she hisses.

"Skye means nothing to me. You, however, do. Don't listen to what she fucking says. You're worth a million more of her."

She hits my chest and scowls. "She's not beneath me. I cook for a living, and she fucks."

I laugh, because it's hard not to when she looks so mad. "In my eyes, no woman is equal to you. You're above every single one of them. You're my Bandia, remember. No one comes close." I press my lips against hers, refusing to move until she opens up and lets me kiss her. When she does, I don't give up until she's melting into me and panting. I'll get shit off the guys, but I'm past caring. When she's in the room, it's only her I see. She wriggles beneath me, and I groan. "Don't play those games, baby, or I'll fuck you right here and I don't care who sees."

She grins, chewing on that bottom lip, all innocent and sexy. She knows what she's doing. I'm contemplating the nearest room with a lock when Grim shouts for me. I know it's serious because he addresses me as 'Pres'.

We call church, and Grim says it needs everyone's attention, so we follow him inside the room and close the door. "Carter is trying to go after Arthur Taylor. Arthur's informant tipped him off right before his warehouse was raided earlier today. Luckily, he got all the weapons out in time, but it was a close call. Now, Arthur is screwing. He wants to meet ASAP."

"Why don't I know about this?" I snap.

"Maybe cos you were too busy screwing the reason we're all in this mess?" growls Crow.

"It's because I turned up to do some work for him right after the raid," says Grim, indicating for Crow to shut up. "He was after blood, so I had to tell him some of what's happened. I gotta warn you, Pres, he ain't too happy about all this."

"Fuck," I hiss. The last thing I need is the Taylors on my back. "Right, set up a meeting."

"He'll pull out the deal," says Crow, "then how will we fund this bullshit with your latest whore?"

I'm too quick when I rush at him this time. No one stops me as my fist crashes against his jaw. He lands in a heap on the floor, spitting blood from his mouth. "I can't take any more of your shit, Crow. I'm done making allowances. You wanna continue hating on me, do it from another club! Don't sit at my table and speak about her like that!"

He grins up at me, his teeth stained red. "If you ain't claiming her, she's open for whatever man."

I hit him again, harder this time. "You touch her and I'll gut you like a fucking fish. She's mine. That goes for any of you fuckers. Rylee is mine, she belongs to me, and I'll kill anyone who tries to take her!"

RYLEE

I gasp, shocked at hearing those words from Maverick. We slept together once and now he's yelling that I'm his? I rush to my room, confused. Why the hell did I pass church at the exact time he screamed those words? Have I escaped one prison for another?

I sit on my bed and go over what I overheard. It was said with such anger and venom, and even though they weren't aimed directly at me, the words still bother me.

When Grant said things like that, it was a threat. I was his and I wasn't allowed to leave. Am I allowed to leave here? Would Maverick refuse to let me go? The thought of being with Maverick, like properly being with him, makes me feel warm inside. If all our days are like last night and today, it wouldn't be a bad thing. But I've just left one relationship, and now, he wants me to jump straight into another.

My bedroom door opens, slamming against the wall. Maverick glares at me. He looks hot when he's pissed. I stare at him, trying to shake the image of us together last night. "I gotta go," he mutters, and I nod. "I don't know when I'll be back."

"Right. You don't have to tell me."

"But I want to." We stare at each other for a few seconds. "Don't be alone with Crow."

I frown. Crow's been kind to me so far, so I don't see him as a threat. Unless this is a way of bossing me around. "Why?"

"Just trust me on this."

"No. I like Crow, and he's nice to me." I'm pushing to see how far his possessiveness goes. Will he get mad if I refuse to stop speaking to people at his request?

Maverick pushes his face into mine, nipping my lip between his teeth. "Nice like I am?" He moves his kisses down my neck, and I close my eyes, trying to find the willpower to push him away.

"Stop," I snap, and he immediately pulls back. "Don't you have somewhere to be?"

A lost look passes over his face before he nods and leaves the room. I stare at the closed door for some time. I'm so confused by his erratic behaviour.

───※───

Nelly tops up my glass. One thing I'm getting used to here is alcohol. Grant would let me drink a glass of wine with dinner when he was in a good mood, but before the MC, I'd never even been drunk. "You lucky bitch."

"It's like when he's around, everything else disappears. I forget about Grant and all the crap surrounding that." Filling her in on my night with Maverick seemed like the thing to do if I want to make good friends here. Nelly is so easy to talk to.

"That's a good thing, right?"

I shrug. "It feels like it. But am I . . . am I jumping out of the frying pan and into the fire?"

She frowns. "Maverick's a good guy, remember?"

"I overheard him earlier, and he was yelling at someone, saying I was his. That no one could touch me. I guess it brings back memories."

"I don't claim to know these guys well. I only got the job a few weeks before I helped you, but I've spent enough time around here to know they are passionate and caring. They're protectors, and I don't get the bad vibes when they say shit like that. Maybe talk to Diamond. Or Brea?"

I nod. "I guess. He told me to stay away from Crow. That pissed me off. I haven't told him to stay away from Skye or Velvet."

"Forget the little things. I wanna know all the other stuff, like how big his—"

"Hey, girls," says Meli, joining us. I smirk at Nelly, who clamps her lips shut. "I'm about to get shit-faced, so if you don't wanna get yourselves into trouble, I suggest you move away from me. Association is almost as bad as the crime around here."

I laugh. I like Meli, and how brave and rebellious she is. "Count me in," I say, and she looks at me surprised. "I wanna forget the world just for a day, and Hadley is watching Disney films with Ella, so I'm free."

CHAPTER TWELVE

MAVERICK

Arthur paces the room. He seems to pace a lot when he's angry. "We gotta end this," he snaps.

"I'm working on it," I reply, "but he's a cop, so we have to do it carefully or we'll end up inside."

"I can't have my business being raided, Maverick," he growls. "People will talk. Clients will lose trust. I have eight fucking shipments due any day. If these bastards are watching, I'll lose millions."

"It won't come to that. I'll strike today."

"Just put a fucking hit out," says Tommy. "It'll solve everyone's problems."

"It'll come back to us or Rylee," says Grim.

"Tell me why I should care about this bitch and her kid," Arthur demands to know. "She doesn't mean shit to me."

"Cos that's gonna be what we do as a club. I thought you were in? You want these women working in your clubs and factories, right? You can't start popping off every battered woman's ex or we're gonna encounter problems. I'll deal with Grant Carter. He won't bother you again."

Arthur sighs. "If he does, I'll take him out, with or without your agreement."

Grim follows me up the garden path. "You sure about this?" he asks for the hundredth time.

I bang on the door, which has been replaced since we had Crow break the lock. It opens and Grant glares at us. "What the fuck do you want?"

"To make a few things clear."

"Be very careful, biker. Turning up at a cop's house, making threats, it could get messy."

"Who's making threats?" asks Grim.

I hand the envelope to Grant, and he hesitates before taking it. "Open it," I push, and he does, taking out the photos and flicking through. "We're ready for the fight. We have evidence of your affair. We have psych reports. We have photographs of her bruises, and it's on record you broke her ribs. If you wanna fight, let's go. But whatever happens, she ain't coming back to you. You've lost. Sign the damn papers and set her free."

Grant smirks, stuffing the pictures back in the envelope and shoving them hard against my chest. "All you got is a bunch of nothing. Men cheat, it's not a crime. I can refuse to sign and she'll have to wait two years for it to go through. Or, she can meet me to discuss things, and I'll consider signing there and then."

"No way. You're not getting near her."

"Scared she might see the error of her ways and come crawling back?"

"She hates you."

"I want to hear that for myself from her mouth."

"No," I say, stepping towards the gate. "It's not happening."

"Then get ready for that fight."

"One more thing," adds Grim. "You know your mistress is pregnant?" Grant's expression shows he didn't have a clue. "You can't beat the shit outta her, can you, with her being a cop and all. Does your boss know about the two of you?" he asks.

"Leave her out of this," he hisses.

"Have a good day, Mr. Carter," I throw over my shoulder. "Oh, and a word of warning, you don't wanna mess with the Taylors. I just had to beg him not to put a hit out on you. I wanna do things right, for Rylee and Ella, but you keep pushing us and it'll be out of my hands."

"That sounded like a threat!" he yells to us as I throw my leg over my bike.

I grin at him before starting the engine. "Just a friendly bit of advice."

***

We get back to the club and I'm fuming. "It wasn't enough," I growl out. Carter won't be shitting himself over that little threat. He's right, we have photographs and nothing else. I head for the office, needing to spend time where I feel closest to Dad. He wouldn't have stood for this back when he was in his prime. I sit in his chair, pour a whiskey from the bottle he kept in his top drawer, and rest my head back, closing my eyes. I need a plan. Now.

4 years earlier...

I glance around the room of sweaty men all cheering and yelling while two of the brothers beat the crap outta each other. I'm thirty years old and I still can't get used to this mindless violence amongst our own. The two men in the make-shift ring are stumbling around, covered in each other's blood, and I'm pretty sure Dad gets off on this sort of shit. I turn away and take a pull on my beer. "Fancy getting out of here and hitting a bar?" asks Grim, and I nod. Fuck this bullshit.

"Grim, get his ass outta the ring," yells Dad. Grim rolls his eyes, without Dad seeing, of course, and steps into the ring to drag out Hawk's passed-out body. "I need some real entertainment," Dad hisses.

"Try watching a real boxing match on the television," I mutter dryly.

"Are you not entertained at all by this?" asks Dad with a grin. He never did get my need to move away from crime and violence. When this place becomes mine, it's the first thing I'm gonna change. "How can a son of mine turn his nose up at a real bare-knuckle fight?" He leers at me.

Crow leers too, never far away from my dad's side. He reminds me of a younger me, trying desperately to get his approval. "Not between my brothers," I say.

"Does it hurt your feelings?" he mocks. I roll my eyes, and it pisses him off, as any show of disrespect does. "Maybe you should step in there," he says, nodding towards the ring.

"No chance," I mutter. He isn't using me for his weird obsession with violence—those days are long gone.

"You wanna run things one day, you gotta learn to fight," he says, and the room begins to quieten down. Brothers begin to watch the altercation, and Dad grins. "We can't have a pussy running shit."

"I can fight," I snap. "I just won't do it for your entertainment."

"Crow would. He's more of a Maverick than you."

"Then let Crow entertain you."

Crow shrugs out of his jacket, showing his willingness to step up, and I smirk. He's like an eager puppy dog. We've never really got on. I spent the first few years of his life hating him. Not because I actually hated him but because Dad did, and I wanted to prove I was behind him one hundred percent. If he was mad, I'd be mad. If he was raging, then so would I. Crow and I naturally kept our distance from one another, and as Crow pushed more into Dad's life, begging for attention, I stepped farther back. It's a good thing—I see things clearer these days and I don't like what I see.

Dad slaps Crow on the back. "Who are you gonna challenge, son?" he asks. Son? Shit, he makes me laugh. Crow shines under his new pet name, but he doesn't see that Dad only says it when he's trying to make him do shit.

Crow looks around the room and his gaze settles on me. "No chance," I say, shaking my head for extra confirmation. Is this kid serious? I'm ten years older than him.

"You're stepping down from a challenge?" Dad smirks.

"Fuck, yeah, he's just a kid."

"He thinks he can take you, so let him try," Dad encourages.

I stare wide-eyed. He's actually serious. He wants me to fight a kid, my own stepbrother. "This is stupid," I mutter.

"No son of mine would dare walk away from a fight!" Dad growls.

"Jesus, just fucking hit him, send him down, and we can go," mutters Grim from beside me.

"Crow, I can't fight you. You're my brother!"

"Stepbrother," Dad interjects. He never misses an opportunity to remind all of us of Mum's mistake.

"I'll go easy on yah," sniggers Crow, and a few of the guys laugh.

"Man, you can't walk away from this," Grim hisses in my ear. "Hit the little shit. You've been desperate to for years."

Crow's a leery little bastard, but I've never wanted to hurt him. It ain't his fault he was brought into this crazy, fucked-up place. I groan, shrugging out of my jacket. I'll let him get a few hits in, then I'll walk away. Losing is better than turning down the fight.

"We need an incentive," announces Dad. Of course, he'd think of that because he's probably guessed I plan on walking away without marking Crow. "Grim, go get me Rosey," he adds, and I ball my fists.

Rosey, her club name on account of her pale English rose complexion and dark red hair, is the daughter of a club whore here, and now she's twenty-one, Rosey is moving the same way. Only right now, she hasn't been touched. I've loved Rosey from the day she turned sixteen. Her mum took her for a makeover and boy did she glow up! All the guys said it. That's when I really noticed her, but I was twenty-five and keeping my distance because of the age difference. We've been spending a lot of time together, and Dad hates that. Just like Crow does, because of course, he's gonna fancy Rosey... who doesn't?

"Fuck you," I hiss, and Dad grins wider.

Grim returns with Rosey, and Dad takes her by the hand. "The winner will get the pure and beautiful Rosey."

Rosey looks terrified. She knew she'd one day become like her mum, but I don't think she was expecting this. "Me?" she squeaks, her eyes wide.

Dad runs his hand over her arse, and I resist the strong urge to rip his head off. "You know the rules, baby girl. You earn your keep, and I'm *doing you a favour by letting your first time be with one of my boys."*

Rosey glances at me nervously.

I get into the ring, where Crow's smiling like a maniac. The bell rings before I've got to my corner and as I turn, Crow catches me off guard, hitting me with a good right hook. I shake my head. Little fucker's acting like his life depends on this bullshit fight. I dodge the next few punches. The brothers are crying out for blood, and I wonder when they all became such vicious animals.

"Are you gonna hit me or not, pussy?" hisses Crow.

"You're twenty years old," I snap.

"Won't stop me fucking that redhead, though." He grins, baiting me. "I know you like her."

"Grow up." I dodge another attempt.

"I'm gonna hold her down and fuck her so hard, she'll never wanna fuck again."

"Boy, you couldn't fuck a ninety-year-old hag. You're a kid."

Crow laughs, surprising me again with a left and catching my cheek. "I bet she likes it up the arse. I might ask Ripper to join me."

I punch him hard enough to make him stumble back. Everyone goes wild and it makes me feel worse. He hisses, giving his eye a rub before straightening up again and shaking it off. Dad taught him well. "Maybe we could get a train going on her. A few of the brothers taking turns, fucking her in every hole."

I lose it, pummelling into his face until he's on the ground, desperately trying to cover his head to avoid the blows. I hear a cry from Rosey and stop. She hates violence, and one glance at her face tells me she's never gonna look at me the same way again.

I get up and storm from the ring, grabbing my jacket from Grim. "Well done, son," Dad congratulates me. He pushes Rosey to me, and I catch her round the waist, but she takes a step back. She can't even look at me.

"Where do you go when you're so lost in thought, you don't hear me calling your name?" asks Hadley, entering my office. Her eyes fall to the whiskey. "Bad day?"

"What can I do for yah, Hads?" I ask. I haven't thought about Rosey for years. What the fuck got me thinking about her today?

"Just checking you're okay. Did you see Grant Carter today?"

I nod. "He wants to meet with her before he'll sign any papers."

"I've got more bad news. The judge wouldn't grant Rylee an injunction. He said there wasn't enough evidence of abuse or violence. It means we can't keep him away from her."

"Course he did. Protecting his own. It wouldn't have made a difference anyway—Carter wouldn't listen to a court order. He's hell-bent on getting her back. I just can't work out why. He's got a new girl with a kid on the way. What's his obsession with Rylee?"

"Just that," Hadley shrugs, "he's obsessed. Men like him don't stop until . . ." she trails off.

"That's my worry." I pinch the bridge of my nose. "Dad would know what to do."

"Dad wouldn't protect a woman like this."

"But he'd know how to sort slippery little fuckers like Carter."

"With illegal means. We can all think of illegal ways to rid the world of men like Carter, but we're doing this right. Sometimes the right way takes longer."

RYLEE

Skye sits beside me. Everyone else seems to have spread out into their own conversations, and Hadley's gone to see Maverick. He returned an hour ago and hasn't come near me. "We all saw your little PDA," she mutters, picking at the grass.

"My what?" I ask.

"Public display of affection, with Mav."

"Oh."

"Just remember what I told you. I'd hate to see you embarrass yourself. Men like him change women like underwear."

"Right. Thanks.

"And he hinted I was in his bed tonight so . . ." she trails off.

"When?" I ask, sitting up straighter.

She smirks. "Oh my god, you're too cute. Did you think he was like your boyfriend or something? These bikers don't stay faithful to one woman. That's what I've been trying to tell you. He practically groped me when I went to the bar, and that usually means he wants a night with me." She stares off dreamily. "I hope Grim's there too."

"What's it like?" I ask. Not because I dream of screwing them both, especially not at the same time, but a sick part of me wants to torture myself and compare how Maverick is with me to her. I guess deep down, I want reassurance that he's different when he's with me.

She smiles. "Mav is so gentle and caring. He takes his time to take care of me. Grim, he's a machine. That's why I love having them together. Mav cuddles up to me after a hard night with Grim. They're the perfect team."

I stand, brushing the grass from me. I never get mad, but right now, I feel raging anger boiling in the pit of my stomach. Who the fuck does he think he is, making a fool outta me? Like I haven't been through enough. Why did I think I was special? I'm an idiot. I march into the club and stop at the bar. I really should go to bed, but I'm too fired up. "Shot," I order, and Crow arches a brow as he places a shot glass before me and fills it with a clear liquid. I knock it back and instantly cough. "What the fuck is that?"

"Careful, Rylee, you're starting to sound like the whores with your sailor language."

"Well, maybe I am like the whores, Crow. I certainly feel like one right now."

"Does this have anything to do with you and Pres, by any chance?" he asks, topping up my glass.

"I don't want to talk about it," I snap, drinking the second shot. I take the bottle from him and top my glass myself. "I know I'm not special. I don't know how to flirt or even recognise when a man tries to flirt with me, but I'm not completely stupid. And I feel like we had this . . . connection." I drink another shot. "He ignored me for weeks, so when he started being all nice, I just thought maybe he felt the same." I take a breath and release it slowly. "Maybe I was just seeing what I wanted to see. Maybe I was looking for a distraction." I bury my face in my hands and growl. "Sorry. You don't wanna hear this."

"No, carry on. Any chance I get to hear shit about him makes my day."

I let my hands drop to the bar and take in Crow's amused face. "Why do you hate him so much?"

"There's too much to list, sweetheart. I don't wanna soil your mind with the images."

"It can't be that bad."

He laughs, but it's void of any humour. "You have no idea about the real Maverick. He lets you see what you wanna see and nothing more. The rest is hidden under fakeness."

"Are you allowed to talk crap about your President?" I tease.

"He'll never be my President. Eagle was and always will be my President."

"Why'd yah stick around if you hate him so much?"

"Hadley and Meli. My mum. He won't be in charge forever, then I'll take my rightful place as President, and I'll run this club just how Eagle wanted it to run."

"And how was that?"

"Well, put it this way, sweetheart, your ex wouldn't be alive right now if I was in charge." He takes the shot bottle from me and places it back on the shelf. "Now, go and get some sleep." He's watching behind me, and I turn to find Skye disappearing into Maverick's office.

"I've spent most of my adult life being told what to do by men," I say, making my way behind the bar. "I'm not ready to sleep." I snatch the bottle back and pour some directly into my mouth. Crow laughs, and I smile. "Your turn," I whisper, holding the bottle to his lips. He lets me pour some into his mouth.

"What the fuck is going on?" yells Maverick, and the bottle jerks, tipping some of the contents down Crow's chin. "Get your hands off her now!" he growls, and I realise Crow's got a hand on my waist. He sniggers, dropping his hand and taking the bottle from me.

"For a second there, sweetheart, I thought you were getting brave." Crow places the bottle on the shelf, and as he passes me to leave, he presses his mouth to my ear. "Remember, don't let him boss you around."

CHAPTER THIRTEEN

MAVERICK

I glare at Rylee, but there's something different about her tonight. She doesn't wilt under my angry stare. Instead, she squares her shoulders, and I almost crack a smile. *There's my goddess. My Bandia.*

"You drunk?" I ask.

"Yes," she hisses, "I am."

"Right, well, you want me to help you to bed?"

"No," she snaps, turning her back to me and grabbing a bottle of tequila. I wince as she takes a few large glugs. When she swallows it, she visibly gags, and I bite my lip to stop the smile escaping. "I want to get so drunk, I don't know my own name. Or yours. Or Grant's. Or anyone else's."

"Riiiight," I say, dragging the word out. "Any particular reason for that?"

"No." She goes to take another drink but pulls the bottle away when she remembers how it tastes. She screws her face up and places it on the bar. "Don't you have things to do?"

I take a seat. She's got something on her mind, and I intend to get to the bottom of it. "I'd rather be here with you."

"Yeah, right."

"Call me paranoid, Bandia, but I feel like you're mad at me."

She scoffs. "Of course, you'd think this was about you."

"It's not about me?" I ask, raising my brows in an 'are you sure' kind of way.

"I saw her," she snaps. "Going into your office. Is she in there now? Won't she wonder where you are?"

"So, it is about me?"

"It's about her. You and her."

I smile. "Are you jealous?"

"No. God, no. Why would you ever think I'd be jealous? I mean, it isn't like we're a thing . . . like we have a connection."

"Right." I nod. "And who do you think is waiting for me in my office?"

"You don't have to pretend. I know you bikers like women . . . a lot. I just don't wanna share." She pauses and confusion passes on her face. "But that's what you like, isn't it? You like to share." She seems to ponder her words before adding, "And I don't. So, it would never work anyway. Oh god," she covers her face, "it'd never work." She begins to pace, and I watch in amusement. "It's okay to have a rebound, isn't it? That doesn't make me a whore. I don't mean in the club sense, I mean just a general whore. Because there's only ever been two people and I've never cheated on anyone."

I reach across the bar and gently take her wrist. She stops pacing, and I pull her closer to me. "Slow down. I don't know what the fuck you're talking about."

Rylee stares at me for the longest time, a range of emotions storming in her eyes. Then she suddenly grabs my face and kisses me. She kisses me like she's starved for me and only me. My dick gets hard instantly, but then she pulls away and groans. "See, I tell myself no . . . no, Rylee . . . you're not an idiot. He reeled you in. But then I go and do that. It's like I can't resist you. This must be what crack addicts feel like, addicted to the drug . . . and you're my drug. You're my crack!" I can't help it, I laugh, amused by her drunken rambling. "Don't laugh at me," she wails, pulling free from me and stepping back so she's out of my reach.

"You're making it impossible for me to take you seriously right now," I say, slowly rounding the bar. She eyes me cautiously as I step into her space. "You arguing with yourself is the cutest damn thing I've ever seen."

"I wasn't trying to be cute," she mutters.

"And then you go and kiss me like that, and you got me thinking all kinds of naughty things." I glance down at my obvious erection, and she blushes as her eyes follow my lead. "But you're crazy drunk, and once that tequila hits, you're gonna pass out. So, you've got ten seconds to tell me what I did wrong. And I know you find it hard to say when you're upset, but I won't punish you for talking truths, Bandia. I might reward you, but I'll never fucking punish you."

She swallows and her eyes water. "Are you having sex with other women?"

"No," I say firmly, keeping her eye contact. "Just you."

"Skye said . . ." she pauses and looks towards my office.

"That's who you saw going to my office?" I ask, and she nods. I take her hand and lead her towards the office door. We can hear moaning coming from inside, and I roll my eyes. I shove the door open with a loud bang, and Skye looks over her shoulder at us from where she's riding Grim. He smirks, and neither stop to explain why the fuck they're in my office again. I close the door, vowing to deal with Grim later because if I do it now, he'll make some shit joke about us joining them. I don't need Rylee setting off again.

"Yah see?" I brush some hair from her face. "I'm not fucking Skye or any other woman in this place. Just you, baby."

"She said you like to join them."

Anger boils inside. It ain't a new thing for club whores to cause drama, in fact, it's almost expected, but not with Rylee. Not when she's been to hell and back. "What else has she been filling your head with?"

"That you groped her earlier today. But it's not just her," she mutters. "I heard you earlier tell someone I'm yours. No one can touch me." I groan, realising she heard me losing my shit with Crow earlier. "I'm not a possession. I've spent too long living like that."

"That's not what I meant," I explain.

"What's even in there?" she asks, staring at the door to where we hold church. Women never go in there, but today, I make an exception. I don't want secrets between us, and I want her to trust me. Unlocking the door, we step inside and she stares at the large oak table. "This is it? This is where you all disappear for hours?"

"What were you expecting?" I ask.

She runs her hand along the table until she gets to my chair. It's bigger than the others and carved with snakes running along the back. "I dunno. Maybe some secret cinema room or a gaming room." She smiles.

"When I said that earlier today, I was just mad," I explain.

"So, I'm not yours?" she asks, trailing her fingers over my chair. "Anyone can touch me?"

Jealousy rips through my chest at the thought of my brothers touching her. I shake my head, following her around the table. "Nobody in my club can touch you."

"Why?"

"There's rules here, Bandia. Certain things are expected. I don't always agree with them, but it's just the way it's always been." She continues around the table, but I stop at my chair. "I'm the President. It gives me an advantage. If I tell the men you're mine, they're not allowed to go near you, not in that way at least."

"What if I want them to?"

"It doesn't matter what you want. They know the rules. What I say goes."

"You must feel so powerful," she mutters.

"I've never claimed a woman, Rylee. I never agreed with it. Who am I to lay claim? We're all free, right? But I don't think I totally understood what it felt like to meet that one person who would make me wanna kill all my brothers." I take a deep breath, giving myself a second to get the words right. "When a biker lays claim, it means he'd lay down his life for that one person above all others. It means he'd do whatever it takes to keep that pretty smile on his woman's face. It means he'll serve her until his last dying breath." I run my hands over my face. "When a biker tells his brothers he's laying claim, it isn't done lightly. I'm not like Grant. I'd never intentionally hurt you and I'd rather slit my own throat than lay a hand on you in anger. When he said you were his, he was treating you like his possession. No one was allowed to look at you or talk to you. He kept you locked away from the world and took pleasure in causing you so much pain. I'd never do that." I make sure I look her in the eye before I say my next words because I need her to believe me. "If you told me you wanted to leave, I'd let you. I'd never make you stay, and while it'd kill me to watch you go, I wouldn't stop you because you're not my prisoner. You're my equal . . . damn it, you're above me.

"You might not see it, but you're in charge, Rylee. I have to warn my brothers off because having this many men living under one roof is like a pack of hungry wolves. They're all sniffing around for a good woman, and if I don't claim you, one of them might and I'd kill him. I'd have to."

"All sounds a bit cult-like to me," she mumbles, moving closer.

"You try living with a bunch of guys with no rules. Becoming someone's ol' lady is an honour, especially to the President. Why'd yah think the whores hang around? It's what they want, to be a part of our family. I wanna build that, Rylee. And I'm not putting this on you, so please don't think I'm crazy, but I want a club full of ol' ladies, kids running around, and a community spirit. My visions for this place are nothing like my dad's. I wish I could tell you all the shit he did. He's the reason I wanna help women who are stuck in abusive relationships."

"He hurt your mum?"

"She hurt him to start with, and I spent years justifying how he treated her because she made one mistake. I was wrong for siding with him, and he was wrong for allowing it. He kept her around to torture her mentally, and he kept Crow around as a reminder. The whole thing was fucked up."

"She had an affair," whispers Rylee, and I nod.

"With his Vice President. You know what that does to a man? It makes him mistrusting, paranoid, and fucked in the head." I spit out the words and lower into my chair. "We all got punished in some way. From that day on, all our lives changed."

"What happened to his VP?" she asks, pulling herself to sit on the table. Her skirt rides up a little and it distracts me. I run my finger over her knee.

"He died."

"Oh, bet Crow was devastated?"

"He never got to meet him. He died before he was born."

I run my hand further up her leg, and she watches me. "So, you're not having sex with anyone but me . . . you've warned your men off me . . . what does that mean for us?"

I use my free hand to part her legs slightly and stroke her inner thigh. "What do you want it to mean?" I brush my finger over her panties, and she gasps. Gripping her hips, I slide her in front of me. "I don't want to rush you. You've just come from a serious relationship."

I press my hand against her chest until she lies back on the table. Placing her feet on my knees, I spread her legs farther apart. I stare at the wet patch on her panties and rub my thumb over it, causing her to sigh in pleasure. "I'm waiting, Rylee," I add.

"I want you," she whispers.

"Easy to say when you're lying on my table like my last meal," I say, grinning. I pull her panties to one side and rub my thumb in circles over her swollen bud. "It's possible I'm just your rebound," I add, leaning closer and inhaling her heavenly scent.

"How will I know?" she asks.

I press my tongue against her and lap her juices. She cries out. "You won't," I whisper, pushing a finger into her, "but I've had my heart broken before, and for you, I'm willing to risk it again."

RYLEE

This is not the way to be strong. I grip Mav's head between my thighs, tugging slightly on his hair as he brings me to orgasm with his skilful mouth. I was certain I'd put him in his place and feel like a powerful queen, but after hearing his words tonight, I know it's too late—I'm so lost in him, there's no way out. I stare at the ceiling, panting so hard, I feel dizzy. How the fuck does he know how to do that? "When was your first time?" I ask.

"You really wanna talk first times when I've still got a hard-on stronger than steel?" he asks, standing between my legs. I reach down to remove my panties, but he stills my hands, shaking his head. "No condom," he explains. He sits back in his chair, and I sit up to stare at his beautiful face.

"How old were you?"

"Young," he answers, rearranging his jeans to allow for his cock. I smirk. Maybe it's the drink, but I'm feeling brazen, so I hop down from the table and kiss him. Reaching for his belt, I loosen it as I work my tongue into his mouth. I drop to my knees, and he smirks, lifting his arse up slightly so I can tug his jeans down a little. He watches with interest as I free his erection and stare wide-eyed. No wonder I was sore after we had sex.

"I wanna know how young," I say, and he laughs.

"Too young to be fucking anything. Too young to realise what I was doing. Too young to realise how to do it."

"I was twelve," I admit before gripping his shaft with both hands and running my tongue along the underside. Mav hisses, throwing his head back.

"I don't wanna know how old you were," he mutters.

I roll my tongue around the head. Mav's grip tightens on the arms of the chair. It feels good to have power over him. I close my lips around the head and slowly take him into my mouth. I take him as far as I can, then release him. "How many?"

"How many what?" he asks. He sounds irritated with my questions. "There's only one thing I want to see coming out of your mouth right now and it isn't words," he mutters, and I grin.

"How many women have there been?" I suck him into my mouth again, and this time, I take him deeper until he hits the back of my throat.

"Fuuuck," he growls. He stares down at me, and I give him my best innocent eyes, hollowing out my cheeks and working my mouth on him. "Now's not the time, baby."

I let him pop from my mouth, and he groans in frustration. "It's the perfect time if you want me to continue."

"Fine. I don't know."

I gasp. "You don't know how many?"

"I've always been careful," he adds.

"Well, you must have a rough idea. Five? Ten?"

"Ah, come on, baby, we're getting into a good rhythm here," he begs. I smirk, flicking my tongue to lick away the build-up of precum. "Over fifty . . . ish. Maybe . . ."

"Wow," I gasp. "You really have lived the life of a biker."

"I'm not proud."

"I bet," I mutter.

He grips his cock and moves his hand up and down. I watch him for a second before closing my mouth over him again. This time, I suck him like he's my favourite lollipop, and even when he hits the back of my throat and causes me to gag, I don't stop. Squeezing his eyes shut, his legs begin to tremble and he runs a hand through my hair.

"Baby, I'm gonna come," he pants. I connect my eyes with his and push his cock in further. When it's clear I'm not gonna stop, he tangles his fingers in my hair and thrusts slightly, reaching his orgasm and coming on a growl. His orgasm rolls for a few seconds before his final thrust. He releases my hair and sags back in the chair, looking completely spent. I lay my head against his leg, and he strokes my hair. If I live like this forever, I'll die a happy woman.

CHAPTER FOURTEEN

MAVERICK

Once my legs have returned from their jelly state, I scoop Rylee in my arms and carry her upstairs. As we leave the room, a few of the guys snigger. I wasn't exactly quiet.

I lay her in her bed and pull the sheets over. "I'll be back." Looking exhausted, she doesn't respond.

I bust into my office like a storm, and Grim looks up in shock. Skye smirks like she thinks I'm here for fun. "You wanna explain why you're talking shit to Rylee?" I growl, and her smirk fades quickly.

"Man, do you mind? I'm almost there," groans Grim.

"I've told you before about using my fucking office," I yell. "Put your damn clothes on."

"Are you serious?" he asks.

"Fucking deadly," I hiss.

Grim tucks himself away, and Skye stands, completely naked, with her hands on her hips. "What's Little Miss Innocent been saying?"

"Your sass is not needed right now, Skye," I growl. "You keep causing me drama, I'll throw you out myself. I didn't want you here in the first place, so I have no problems sending you packing."

"I was helping her out!" she snaps.

"By lying? By telling her I'm fucking you?"

"You almost did, and it's only a matter of time, let's be honest."

"Darling, I wouldn't touch you if you were the last human on this planet and my life depended on it. Stay the fuck away from Rylee. You upset her and you're gone." I turn to Grim, who looks pissed. "And you need to confine this shit to your room."

He shakes his head, his eyes full of disappointment as he passes me. "I remember when you were fun to hang out with, brother. This place is changing you back to that eager little boy who lived to please his psycho dad. Be careful or you'll end up as twisted as him."

"It's fucking Pres!" I yell to his retreating back.

Instead of joining Rylee, I decide to head out on my bike. I need the road to get my head straight, but before I know it, I'm stopping at Arthur Taylor's nightclub. Stepping off my bike, I stare at the floods of people waiting to get in. A year ago, this was my life—clubbing, drinking, using women. And now, I'm facing more responsibility than I ever have.

"What brings you here?" asks Tommy, stepping away from the doors and approaching me with his hand out. I shake it firmly.

"Needed a change of scenery," I say.

He smiles. "You chose the right place. Step inside, I'll take you upstairs."

The place is swanky. Grim would hate it. Upstairs is a private floor, but the beats from the club still ring out in a low tone, and there's floor-to-ceiling windows looking out over the lower floor. There's a table in the centre similar to our church table. Arthur is at the head of it with a few other men scattered around. "Found him outside making the place look untidy," explains Tommy.

Arthur stands and shakes my hand. "You got any news for me?" he asks.

I shake my head. "Not really. I saw him, threatened him, but I don't think he took it on board. I'm out of ideas."

I sit down at the table. "Do you play?" he asks, pointing at the poker cards. I shake my head, and he throws his cards in. "Me either, I'm losing." He tells the other men to call it a night and they leave. "Why'd yah come to me, Maverick? You wanna run things legal, and I don't, so how the fuck are we working together?"

I smirk. "Everyone needs a mobster in their life."

"I heard how your dad ran that club. He was notorious back in the day."

"It's ultimately what killed him. I'm nothing like him."

"I see that. Bet he hated it."

A waiter sets a drink in front of me. "I was different back then. A mini version of him."

"What's your vision for that club of yours? Cos, I like you, Maverick. Something about you makes me wanna join forces permanently. I like the way your men work. They're good at what they do, and they get results. I haven't had a missed payment in weeks."

"Glad to hear it." I pause to take a drink. "I wanna help women like Rylee," I say. "I've sorted out rooms and I wanna give them a place to stay."

"How are you gonna help all those women? You can't save everyone."

"I thought I could build up some of our businesses again, get them work so they can become independent."

"Nice in theory," he mutters. He finishes his drink, and the waiter tops it right back up. "I'm not saying it's a bad idea. You could be on to something, but the way I hear it, your businesses aren't doing great. I know we spoke of the women getting jobs in my businesses, but do you want them working for someone like me?"

"Rylee has no paperwork. No forms of identity. Lots of women will leave their homes with nothing, just like her. They'll need cash-in-hand work until we can get their paperwork together. That's where you'll come in. And yeah, my businesses aren't doing great. No one wants to use a garage that's run the honest way no more. They see the modern places that rip them off and go there, dazzled by salesmen and shiny windows. Our customers are older than the fucking Queen. Men loyal to Dad. Once that generation drops dead, we'll have nobody."

"Lucky for you, business is my specialty." He smirks. "Yah know, the land the garage sits on is worth a lot of money. You could sell it. A clever businessman would pay a lot for it. It's literally a walk away from some of the trendiest bars."

"I can't sell it," I mutter, rubbing my brow.

"Mav, you're not hearing me. It's worth half a mill, easy."

"You're not hearing me. I *can't* sell it. It hides too many of my father's sins."

RYLEE

I wake as Mav creeps into my bed. "Sorry," he whispers, wobbling as he dives under the sheets.

"Are you drunk?"

"Are you?" he counters.

I check the time—it's almost five in the morning. "Where have you been?"

He snuggles against me. "Just be happy I'm here with you," he mumbles against my neck.

I frown. "What the hell does that mean?"

"I've been making deals with the devil."

I turn onto my side so we're face-to-face. "Oh yeah, did you tell him I said hi?"

He smirks. "Baby, goddesses go to heaven. You'll never say hi to the devil."

I watch him fall into a restless sleep. He flinches and mumbles, occasionally jerking. I stroke my fingers gently over his muscled chest, and he relaxes. I can't help but wonder why he looks so troubled when he's sleeping. I want to be the one to take his troubles away.

∞

Maverick is grumpy when he's hungover. I've been sitting with Hadley on the couch for half an hour and all we've heard is yelling. When Ghost storms out of Grim's office, Hadley shrugs. "Maybe they've fucked something up?"

"Maybe he's pulling rank. I feel like he was getting sick of the guys being tardy."

Hadley laughs. "Who says tardy under the age of ninety?"

I grin. "I haven't seen much of Meli today."

"She hides away when Ripper is on Meli watch. She really hates him. More than anyone else here."

"I got that impression. She almost had a fit the other day when she saw Ripper playing with Ella. She acts really weird around him."

"That's why Dad always made him watch over her. It was the only time she behaved." Hadley smiles, but then something troubles her and she frowns. "Saying that out loud—"

"Yeah, I thought the same," I cut in. We stand at the same time, and I scoop Ella up in my arms. Something about the Meli and Ripper situation rings alarm bells.

We find Meli in her room, and she looks at us with amusement. "Okay, what's going on?"

"Nothing," I say innocently. "We just thought we'd check on you."

"I'm hungover and hiding out."

Ella sits on the floor and sets out her colouring. "We could hit the bar again tonight," I say, ignoring the vomit threatening to rise at the thought of drinking, "Ripper offered to watch Ella for me," I lie.

Meli's eyes bug out of her head. "No."

"Why?" I ask.

"I don't want to drink."

"I don't mind joining you," offers Hadley.

"Then I'll watch Ella," says Meli.

"You'd rather babysit than drink with us?" asks Hadley. "Something's not right."

Meli shuffles her magazines into a messy pile. "I told you, I'm hungover."

"Hair of the dog then," I say, rising to my feet. "I'll check if he's still okay to watch her."

Meli presses herself against the door and shakes her head. She looks scared, and my face softens. "Mel, what's going on?" She worries her lower lip, and I know she wants to talk but something stops her. "Fine, I'll ask him myself."

She panics. "No, don't do that!"

"Have you two had some sort of fling?" asks Hadley, screwing her face up. Ripper is one of the original members of the club. He must be in his fifties.

"No," whispers Meli, staring at her feet.

"Maybe not a fling," I begin, and her eyes meet mine, "but he's hurt you." I know that look because it haunts me whenever I stare into the mirror. "Mentally and physically," I guess.

"Mel, has Ripper hurt you?" asks Hadley, standing beside me.

Meli's eyes water and a stray tear slips down her cheek. "Don't say anything," she whispers. "You can't tell anyone."

"How? When? Oh my god." Hadley drops back down on the bed. "I don't understand."

"It's done now. I've moved forward," Meli insists. I tuck her hair behind her ear and smile sadly. "Dad found out and put a stop to it. Back then, it wasn't such a big thing, not like nowadays."

"It's never been okay," I whisper. "They might have made you feel like that, but it's not."

"Meli, you have to tell Mav," says Hadley, and Meli panics again, shaking her head and pressing herself harder against the door. "He'll kill him when he finds out."

"It's over. It was dealt with. You know how Mav gets after he's killed someone," she hisses, and that takes me by surprise. I never imagined Maverick could kill anyone. The girls don't notice my horror as they continue in hushed tones. "I can't be responsible for sending him spiralling. I don't want it all dragging back up again."

Hadley takes a deep breath. "It was when you were fifteen, wasn't it? You changed overnight, and I couldn't work it out."

"I was fifteen when Dad found out," admits Meli. "But it started way before then. I was eleven . . . maybe younger. I remember him paying me special attention right from when I was a little girl."

My stomach rolls. I've let this man around my daughter. Never alone but still. "What did your dad do?"

Meli shrugs with a faraway look in her eyes. "He said I shouldn't dress like a whore and then men wouldn't look at me like that." A sob escapes Hadley and she slams her hand over her mouth. "It just made me behave even worse. What was the point if he was gonna make excuses like that? Truth is, I wasn't dressing any different to any other teenage girl." She offers Hadley a watery smile. "Except you, Hads." Hadley returns the smile. "Dad just told me it was dealt with, and after that, Ripper left me alone. He still leers at me with that nasty smile, but he hasn't touched me."

"Oh, sweetie." I pull her in for a tight hug, and she lets me. Hadley joins us.

"I always thought you hated me," mumbles Hadley. "You stopped talking and sitting in my room to watch films."

"I didn't hate you, Hads. I was scared he'd turn to you if I wasn't in my room when he expected me to be. I didn't want him to hurt you."

It breaks my heart, and I hug them tighter. Maverick really would kill Ripper if he knew, and I hate that I can't tell him.

CHAPTER FIFTEEN

MAVERICK

Grim's still in a pissy mood with me, but I'm hungover and I need to talk to him, so when I call him into my office and he drops in the chair like a teenager, I can't help but laugh. "It's simple. Fuck who you want in your own space, not mine."

"Get on with the lecture," he mutters.

"Grim, I don't wanna be like this. I don't want to be yelling and reading everyone the riot act. But you guys need to help me out a little. I don't know what the fuck I'm doing around here, and I feel like I'm doing it by myself!"

"I told you we shouldn't have come back here."

"How could I not? You imagine leaving this place to Crow?" Grim sniggers. "Look, I need you, man. That's why I made you Vice President."

He sits up and nods. "Right, fine, pull at the heartstrings, why don't yah."

"I went to Arthur's nightclub last night. You know his weekend turnover is more than our monthly turnover?"

"He's a businessman."

"And you aced business studies. Don't mean shit unless you're clever. He told me to sell the land under the garage."

Grim laughs. "So the new owner can build a haunted house?"

"I told him." Grim's eyes bug out of his head. "I trust him," I add. "So, he offered to buy it."

"You seriously wanna sell that place? Crow will have a shit-fit."

"Crow can kiss my arse. I'm sick of him and his negative attitude to everything I do. That's why I need you on side for this, man. The Perished Riders MC needs to move with the times."

"I agree with you, brother. I always have your back, but just get ready for the showdown cos you know there'll be one."

"Well, let's go to church and get it over and done with."

I lay the accounts book open in the centre of the table. It's all there for the men to see. The business is breaking us and sucking us dry. "When Eagle opened the garage, it was thriving," I begin. "He built up a place using his skill as a mechanic and had some loyal customers. But these days, it's falling apart. The building needs demolishing and rebuilding. Business is barely scraping us by, and it's costing us more to keep it open."

"What are you saying?" asks Copper.

"I think it's time we admitted defeat and cut it loose."

"No way!" yells Crow, diving up from his seat.

"Sit the fuck down," I order.

"I don't mean to piss on your fire, Pres, but there's a reason we've clung on to that building," says Ripper.

"I know. That's why I've found a discreet buyer."

"You've made the decision already, why are you bringing it to the table?" snaps Crow.

"I haven't made a decision. That's not down to just me, but I wanted to make sure I had everything in place to give you the right information. Last week, the garage pulled in three grand. It costs us more to keep it open and pay wages. When Dad opened it, we used it to clean dirty money. Those days are gone. It doesn't work as a legit business."

"So, what are you proposing?" asks Lock.

"We sell to my buyer. We need the land valued, but he seems to think it's worth half a mill." The men glance at each other. "With that kind of money, we can open a better business. We can make use of our skills. Tatts, we could open a shop for you to do ink. Dice, you'd be great in a micro pub with an underground casino. The possibilities are endless."

"It sounds good," says Copper, and Grim nods in agreement.

"We'll be wiping out the last of Eagle," mutters Crow.

"Good," I say bluntly, and everyone stares wide-eyed. "Why are we pretending he was our hero? We all know what he was capable of, what sort of things he did. What he wiped under the carpet," I say, staring at Crow pointedly. "We don't even know why he died or who the fuck killed him. He was shady and he hid shit from us. We have no leads because he kept shit to himself. Who knows what he was fucking planning? He ran this place into the ground, and he'd have left you all homeless. I'm trying my best to save us here."

"Well, I'm in," says Grim.

"Of course, you are," Crow mutters.

"I need a hundred percent votes for this," I say. "I want us all on board."

"You know that won't happen," says Crow.

"Instead of thinking of yourself, think of your brothers, for once," Grim snaps at Crow. "All those in favour, say 'aye'." Everyone votes for. It comes to Crow, and he glares hard at the table. We wait patiently, and he reluctantly mutters 'aye' under his breath. I smile at Grim.

"I'll call the buyer."

Rosey was pissed with me. I left that room and went straight out with Grim. I didn't want my prize for beating Crow's arse, not like that anyway. But two days have passed and Rosey won't speak a word to me. I won so she wouldn't have to give herself to Crow. Staring out from my balcony, it's early evening and the night air is cool, but I welcome it. "Am I not good enough?" I turn around to find her standing in my room. She wobbles on her heels, and I can tell she's drunk.

"What are you talking about?"

"You won and left. You screwed some dirtbag from the nightclub. I heard her fake screams of ecstasy."

I roll my eyes and stare out across the skyline. "You're being ridiculous."

"You should have stayed!" Rosey bursts into tears, and I jump from my seat to comfort her, but she pushes me away. "No. It's too late now."

"I wasn't gonna fuck you because I beat my brother to win you. I beat him so he couldn't fuck you."

"Only he did, so . . ."

I glare at her, my fists balling at my sides. "What?"

"He did fuck me, Mav, so it was pointless."

I scowl. "You let him . . . touch you?"

"No, I didn't let him. He just took it," she yells.

I suck in a deep breath, too stunned to react. "But—"

"He said you cheated by walking out, so he won by default."
"That little fucker. I'll tell the Pres, and he'll kill him."
She scoffs. "He knows, Mav. He knows because he was there."

I jolt upright, looking around like a wild animal. I must have dropped off to sleep out here on my balcony. The pain of Rosey's confession burns in my chest again, and I wonder if it'll ever go. I take a few deep breaths and stand on shaky legs. I need Rylee.

Knocking lightly on her bedroom door, I can hear whispering, so I open it and freeze. Crow grins at me from Rylee's bed. She looks up in surprise, then smiles wide. "Hey, where have you been?" she asks.

"Why are you here?" I ask Crow, ignoring Rylee.

"Just getting the good lady to take a look at my finger," he says, winking at Rylee.

She rolls her eyes. "He cut his finger. I've told him not to use my cooking knives," she says. She rips some tape from a reel and sticks a bandage that's already wrapped around his finger.

"Get out," I snap, and Rylee shifts uncomfortably. "Get the fuck out," I yell when he doesn't move.

Crow slides off the bed. "Thanks, Ry," he says, strutting past me.

I slam the door, causing Ella to cry from the next room. Rylee glares at me before heading to tend to her. When she returns, I'm sitting on her bed with my head in my hands. "I'm sorry," I mutter. "I shouldn't have yelled."

"Last time I checked, you said this was my room." I nod silently. "So, I can have whoever I want in here."

"Except Crow," I say.

"Including Crow. What is your problem with him?"

"Would you be happy if Skye was in my room?"

"Well, no, but that's different. You have a seedy past with her."

"I haven't fucked her once. She's grinded on me, but I've not stuck my dick in any part of her."

"Should I congratulate you on that?" she snaps. "You've been in a pissy mood all day. If you can't handle your hangovers, you shouldn't drink till five in the morning."

"You know I came here cos I needed you," I snap, "but forget it." I storm out the room and head down to the bar. I instantly feel shitty, but I hate how Crow hangs off her and she allows it. She's too nice to see what he's doing.

Grim looks up when I sit beside him. "You can't hack two nights running."

"I managed many times," I say. "You remember when we went to Ireland? Seven days straight we partied."

He grins. "What I'd give to go back to those days."

"I thought about her tonight," I mutter. He hands me his bottle of half-drunk vodka. "I fucking hate that night, but it replays like a broken fucking record."

"It's cos we came back."

"I should have listened to you and ran in the other direction." I take a large gulp, then hand the bottle back. "Wherever she is, I hope she's happy."

"To Rosey," says Grim, waving the bottle in the air before drinking some and passing it back.

"Rosey," I say, doing the same.

RYLEE

It's not the laughing that wakes me but the stumbling around. It sounds like Maverick is banging on every damn wall as he makes his way along the passage. Pulling my bedroom door open, I watch as Grim unhooks Mav's arm from around his neck and steadies him against my door frame. "He's a little drunk." Grim smirks.

"To Rosey," says Mav, clinking an imaginary glass in the air. Grim looks away uncomfortably. I don't know who the fuck Rosey is, but she better not be another club whore.

"You want help getting him to bed?" asks Grim.

I shake my head. I've had plenty of practise with Grant. "You're not coming in here," says Mav. "We're not sharing this one."

Grim laughs as I close the door and guide Mav to my bed. He flops down onto his back in the centre of the bed like a starfish. I stare down at him with my hands on my hips. "I loved her, yah know," he mumbles sleepily. "She was everything." I stiffen. "That's why they did it. To fuck my life up." I kneel and remove his heavy boots. "Why does he hate me so much when he did what he did? I should hate him for stealing my woman."

When I stand, he's snoring lightly. I sigh and head for Ella's bed.

It was Diamond's stupid idea to get fit. She's roped all the women in, even the club girls. We're halfway through the routine when Mav comes out, shading his eyes from the bright sunshine. I left him to sleep, cos he needed it, and now, it's almost lunchtime. I notice Velvet and Skye fix their hair and check the right amount of boob is showing as I watch his masculine frame slowly move in our direction. Playing it cool, I pretend I haven't noticed him and let out a scream when his arms wrap around me from behind.

Maverick pulls me against his front, burying his nose in my hair and inhaling deeply. "I'm such an arse," he grumbles. Skye's eyes burn into me, and I offer a friendly smile. I don't want her to hate me.

"Mav, I'm working out," I whisper.

"I hate waking up when you're not there." He pushes his erection against my arse. "You look hot, by the way."

I smile. "Maybe you want to tell me who Rosey is before you start sweet-talking me." I feel him stiffen, which makes me suspicious. When he doesn't reply, I turn in his arms. "Well?"

"Who the fuck's been discussing my business?" he snaps, and I pull back. I just assumed it was an ex, but the way he's reacting makes me think she's someone I need to be worried about. I turn back to where Diamond is still pumping her arms up in the air and I follow her moves. "Rylee, I asked you a question." His direct tone makes that unsettled feeling appear in the pit of my stomach. When will that fear fade? I know Maverick would never hurt me like that.

"You said her name," I snap, "when you turned up at my room so drunk, I had to remove your shoes and put you to bed. I slept with Ella, by the way, so thanks for that." He moves in front of me, blocking my view of Diamond.

"What did I say?"

"When you tell me who she is, I'll tell you what you said."

We have a few seconds of stand-off, his eyes fixed firmly on mine, but I refuse to look away. I *will* learn not to be scared of every fucking man who challenges me. He huffs, then storms back inside. I'm disappointed he didn't share. How can I trust him one hundred percent when he's reluctant to tell me things?

When the workout is done, I flop down next to Hadley and Meli. "What was up with lover boy?" asks Meli. She seems brighter today, like a weight has been lifted.

"Nothing important," I mumble. Keeping my love life secret is second nature to me. "But I've been thinking. I want to feel more confident. I want to walk down the street and not be petrified that I'll see Grant and he'll hurt me, so I want to learn how to take care of myself."

"Like self-defence?" asks Meli, and I nod. "Sounds good. I'd join you."

"Me too," says Hadley.

I smile. "Great. I'll ask Nelly too. Maybe one of the guys here can teach us?"

Meli groans. "There's only Grim who'll be able to help us with that. He used to do something similar."

I push up from the ground. "I'll go and ask him." Hadley looks even happier to know Grim will be involved. Meli doesn't.

I find Grim in the kitchen with Maverick and Skye. I try not to let it bother me that she's closer to him than she needs to be. He's told me there's nothing between them, and I believe him. He might be secretive, but so far, he hasn't lied to me. "Grim, I need to ask a favour," I say sweetly, and Grim glances at Mav nervously.

"Does he know about it?" asks Grim, tipping his head to Mav.

I shake my head. "No. I've only just discussed it with the girls."

"Is it likely to get me shot?"

I frown. "No, I don't think so. I just wanted some self-defence lessons."

He relaxes and smiles. "Oh, right."

"Why?" asks Mav, looking annoyed.

"So, is that a yes?" I continue as if Mav hasn't spoken.

"I don't have a problem with it," says Grim.

"I fucking might. Why do you want self-defence lessons?" I stare at Mav like he's being dumb, and he huffs again. "But you're safe here."

"So, I can't ever leave these grounds?" I ask. "I want to walk down the street or take Ella to school and not be looking over my shoulder."

"You can do those things, and I'll be with you," says Mav.

"You can't be with me every second." I turn to Grim. "Hadley and Meli want in too and I'm gonna ask Nelly."

"Okay. Just let me know when you're ready and I'll be happy to help."

"I bet you will," grumbles Mav, and Grim laughs.

After my shower, I head into the main room and pause when I see Maverick with Ella, watching a kids' film on the big screen. They look so relaxed together and it warms my heart. I'd have given anything to see Grant with her like this. He never paid her the slightest bit of attention. Since being here, she's really come out of her shell, especially with the guys taking the time out to check she's okay.

I lean against the door frame and watch as Ella climbs onto Mav's knee. She settles against him, resting her head on his chest and placing her tiny hand over his. He smiles to himself, then his eyes land on me, and I hold his gaze for a few seconds before joining them on the couch.

"I'm sorry about yesterday . . . and today," he says.

"It's fine."

"I hate seeing Crow sniffing around you like a fucking bloodhound," he adds, covering Ella's ears.

"Even if he is sniffing around me, I'm not interested," I say.

He scoffs. "That don't always matter to him."

"What's that supposed to mean?"

He shakes his head. "Never mind. Just don't be in closed rooms with him, especially not your bedroom. I don't trust him."

I laugh. "He's your brother."

"Stepbrother. Just trust me on this, he's only doing it to piss me off."

I arch my brow. "Thanks."

"You know what I mean. I've told him to stay away, and he seeks you out even more. He's a dick." He sighs. "And I'm sorry for taking your bed and being so drunk I couldn't take my own shoes off," he adds, and I smile. "It's been a while since I was that carefree. I guess I forgot myself for a night."

"I know you have a lot going on, Mav. But I'm here for you. If you need to offload or just sit in silence, don't feel like you have to protect me. I'm a big girl."

Mav stares down at where Ella's hand entwines with his. "I went to see Grant," he mutters. "He was stepping on my business associate's toes, and I can't allow that, so I went to your house, and I had words. He said he'd sign the papers." I sit up straighter with hope building in my chest. "But on the condition you meet with him. I told him no, but I wanted you to know."

"Why does he want to see me?"

"It don't really matter cos he isn't going to."

"But he might sign the papers. I'll be free."

"You're not seriously considering this," he snaps.

I shrug. "I don't want to see him, the thought terrifies me, but when he signs the papers, I'll be free."

"It won't be that easy and you know that. This is another power trip for him. We'll find another way to sort it all out. I've got a meeting with a solicitor from Hadley's place in half an hour."

"I want to be there," I say, but he shakes his head. "Why do you keep doing this?" I snap. "This is my life, and I want to know what the hell is going on. Stop protecting me."

CHAPTER SIXTEEN

MAVERICK

Rylee slips her hand into mine. It's a small move, but one I love, especially because we've been sniping at one another these last couple of days. The solicitor, Neve Lane, makes a few notes on her laptop, then looks up. "I think we should take this all the way," she announces. "Why the hell should he walk away with the house and everything after what he's put you through?"

"But I don't have evidence," says Rylee.

"That is a shame, and it would have helped a lot, but let's work with what we have. Think back, was there ever a person who heard anything? A scream, a cry for help?"

Rylee nods. "Yeah. Nelly, who was my next-door neighbour. There was also Grant's work partner, Lois Grey. She did a welfare check."

"And she didn't ask if you wanted to press charges?"

She shakes her head. "She's having an affair with him, so no. I'm pretty sure she had sex with him in my living room right after the check."

"Let me get this straight. An officer came to your house to check on you and had sex with your husband, the perpetrator?" asks Neve, and Rylee nods. "Can you remember what date that was?"

"It was the date of the charity day here," says Rylee, looking at me, "I wrote it in my diary, so I have the time and everything," she adds.

"You kept a diary?" asks Neve.

Rylee smiles. "I know it's weird at my age, but it gave me something to do."

"Did you write everything in it?" Neve continues.

"Yes. It's at the house I shared with Grant. Hidden. He didn't know about it because I mainly wrote about him."

Neve stares at me with hopeful eyes. "Any way you can get that for me?" she asks, and I nod. "There's your evidence, Rylee."

"That will stand up in court?" she asks, and Neve nods.

Lock takes a few minutes to pick the lock of the back door in Rylee's old home, then we step inside. The place is a mess, with dirty dishes and takeout cartons strewn all over the kitchen. The living room is just as bad, with empty bottles of wine and cans of beer stacked up. "Looks like the guy's been struggling without Rylee," says Lock.

I stare at the photos of Grant and Rylee together that hang on the wall. She isn't smiling, not fully, and he's got her gripped tight to his side in every one. Heading upstairs, I open each door until I find the bedroom Rylee once shared with that monster. The sheets are crumpled in the centre of the bed. I shift the bedside cabinet and feel the floorboards like she told me to until I find the loose one. Lifting it, I find a shoebox, take it from its hiding spot, and replace everything else.

"There's some toys in here," comes Lock's voice. "Shall I take some for Ella?"

"Yeah, don't disturb anything."

I move to what I think is an en-suite bathroom but find a small storage cupboard. There's handcuffs hanging from a metal bar secured to the wall. I close it hard, sick to my stomach to think he probably put Rylee in there.

We leave and it's like we were never there. I secure the shoebox in my bike parked a few streets away. "I'll meet you at the club," I say to Lock, then I head for the solicitor's office, parking outside and stepping from the bike. I take the diary from the shoebox and take a seat on a nearby wall. I take a deep breath before opening it and skimming through the first few pages.

It doesn't make for pretty reading—rape, regular beatings, tied up, starved. I grind my teeth when I see he locked her out in the garden naked, in the pouring rain, while he ate dinner and made her watch through the window. I slam the diary closed. One day, I'll read it so I can begin to understand what she's been through, but right now, I need Neve to see this.

She does the same as me, flicks through a few pages and raises her brows. "How is she still smiling?" she mutters.

"What do we do now?"

"We report him. Let's get this bastard arrested. One other thing, Mav, I tried to get a copy of Ella's birth certificate and their marriage certificate. The registry office said they don't have anything under those names. Just check with Rylee that I have the correct names and dates, please, and call me."

I nod. "Sure. What does it mean if they can't find them? Can she still divorce him without it?"

"We need to query if they ever existed. Did they ever register Ella's birth? Where did they get married and was it made official in the U.K.? We might not need to pursue the divorce if the marriage doesn't exist. It would explain why he's holding on to the papers. But we still want half of everything. They lived as common-law husband and wife, even if it wasn't official."

Rylee confirms the details Neve has are correct. "Who registered Ella?" I ask.

"He did," says Rylee. "And we got married in Greece."

I pinch the bridge of my nose. "Did you get it registered in this country when you returned?" She shrugs. "Rylee, if you didn't go to a registry office together when you got back, you're not married here, at least not in the eyes of the law." She stares at me in silence. "You might not need those divorce papers signed after all."

"So, I could be free?" I nod, and she releases a shaky breath.

"Neve is calling the police and having the abuse logged. She's pushing for his arrest and a charge of battery."

"Good," she mutters.

"If he's found guilty, he could go to prison. It means you'll be free to walk the streets." I place a kiss on her collarbone. "It'll all be over. And what judge wouldn't grant an injunction order with that diary as evidence?"

"I feel like I can finally breathe," she whispers.

I press my mobile to my ear. "Neve," I greet.

"I just wanted to update you that Grant Carter was arrested, and he's been suspended pending enquiries, but I've just had a call from his solicitor. They want to deal with this on the hush hush

"I bet they do," I snap.

"They're asking if we'd agree to let them deal with Carter internally. He'll face a disciplinary and be placed on probation at work, where they'll watch his every move."

"No fucking way."

She laughs. "I thought you'd say that."

"For some of the shit in that diary, he should go to prison."

"I agree. But they're gonna fight it. He's already saying she was unstable, and that he was worried for her safety. He doesn't know about the diary yet. I'm saving that for when we have to up our game. I've also been to the registry office. There is no registered birth for Ella, so we need to fix that. They're also not legally married in the U.K., so we don't need to pursue the divorce."

"Jesus, it was all fucking smoke and mirrors. He kept her there, making her think she was his wife!"

"You need to prepare Rylee for the road ahead. She'll have to stand up in court and talk about some of the darkest times in her life. Carter's going to have the best lawyers to try and protect his name."

***

I sit on the grass and watch from a distance as the girls surround Grim as he shows them some self-defence moves. He's trained in all things self-defence, and I forgot how good he was at it until now. I smile to myself when the girls give it a go. Grim ends up throwing each of them down, and Meli yells in frustration each time. She'll hate him getting one over on her. When they're done, I tell Rylee to shower. I want to spend some alone time with her, and the only place I'm not gonna get distracted by her flushed face and sexy body is if we go out to eat somewhere.

Rylee looks stunning in a white summer dress that shows off her tanned legs. Since being at the club, she's spent most of her days out in the yard catching the sun. After reading parts of her diary, I can see why.

We're seated by the window in a high-end bar and given menus. Rylee smiles across at me. "It's been a long time since I went out to eat," she says.

"I'll make sure I take you out every week, baby."

"I'm just as happy at the club cooking for you all," she adds with a grin.

"Those men live for your cooking, Rylee. They'll be pissed tonight because I've taken you out."

She laughs. "I saved them some leftovers in the fridge." I roll my eyes playfully. She really takes care of the men, and I love that about her.

We order food, a steak for me and a chicken salad for Rylee, and we opt for soft drinks, both having had enough alcohol recently. We talk about the sale of the garage, and I tell her my plans for some of the money we'll make. She's excited at the thought of helping other women like her and insists on joining me for the meeting with the women's shelter next week. I smile. "It's great to see you so happy and looking forward."

"I just feel so light, knowing this might actually be my real life from now on. I thought I was stuck with Grant forever. I couldn't think of a way to escape him."

"I read some of your diary," I admit, and she lowers her eyes. "I'm sorry, I know I shouldn't have because it's private to you, but I wanted to understand you better."

"And did it help?"

I shake my head. "No. It just puts nasty images in my head and makes me want to hurt that son of a bitch."

She reaches across the table and places her hands over my own. "It's the past. We all have shit we don't wanna talk about, like you and Rosey, and that's okay," she says, her eyes watching me closely for a reaction. I want to tell her about Rosey, there's so much I want to tell her, but I don't want to change how she feels about me, and knowing who I was back then, might. "But know I'll be here, ready, whenever you want to talk."

"Did he lock you in the cupboard in the bedroom?" I ask, changing the subject. The question takes her by surprise, and she gets flustered. "Just . . . I saw the handcuffs and . . ." I leave the sentence hanging.

"Like I said, it's in the past. Grant did all kinds of twisted shit. Whenever I thought it couldn't get any worse, it did. And I can talk about it, if that's what you really want, but going over it with you is like reliving it. I don't wanna see that pitying look in your eyes."

Honestly, I don't think I'm ready to hear all the details spilling from her mouth anyway, so I nod. "Tell me about the wedding," I say.

She laughs nervously. "I thought you were taking me on a date. The first rule is to never talk about your ex. It's date etiquette."

I ignore her. "Were your parents there? You never really talk about them."

"Why would I? I don't have anything to do with them. Christ, Mav, what's going on?"

"These are the kinds of questions they'll ask you in court," I say. "If you can't talk about any of it to me, then how will you stand in a room full of strangers?"

RYLEE

"Court?" I repeat, feeling totally confused and dizzy with his weird questions and his change in mood. He promised me dinner, yet I feel like I'm on the stand now.

"I spoke with Neve," he tells me. "Grant's solicitor wanted to deal with it all hush hush. Said they'd keep an eye on him, put him on probation at work. Obviously, I said no, so Neve is pushing for a hearing. You can send that shithead to prison, but you need to speak about it all."

I shake my head. "Hold on, so you and Neve decided you wanna take this all the way?"

"Well, yeah. It's what you want, right?"

"I don't know because you've literally just sprung it on me. What happened to letting me make my choices, Mav?" We've spoken about it so many times, and I'm angry he's taken it away from me again. I feel ambushed and steamrolled. "You and Neve won't have to stand up in court and relive it, all with him sneering at you. And, actually, he was in line for a sergeant's position, so having him put on probation at work will set his career right back, and that'll hurt him more than anything."

"More than going to prison?" he growls. His face is red through anger, and I can tell he's trying not to yell.

The waitress sets our dinner on the table, and I stare at the salad. I've suddenly lost my appetite. "You have to stop taking control," I mutter. "I know you're helping me, and I'm grateful, but I need to decide what happens next. Not you. Not Neve." I drop my napkin on the table and push to my feet. "I am so incredibly indebted to you for everything you've done and continue to do. I don't want to sound like an ungrateful bitch because I'm not trying to be, but this is huge, and I need to think about it." I head for the door.

"Rylee, where are you going?" He growls, "It's not safe out there."

"Will it ever be?" I ask.

He scrambles around for his wallet as I leave. I need air and I need to get my head straight. I'm almost at the end of the street by the time I hear his heavy boots chasing me down. I glance back as he slows to a walk, staying two steps behind me, and I smile to myself. He's giving me my space but still keeping me safe. I spot a park and head for it. There are couples walking hand-in-hand, taking an evening stroll. They look happy, but then so did Grant and I to the outside world. I find a quiet spot under a tree and take a seat, and Maverick moves nearby but leaves a good gap.

"I shouldn't have walked out on dinner," I eventually admit.

"I'm so used to making decisions, to taking control. I do it automatically."

"I know. You were looking out for me, and I get it. I want him to pay for what he put me and Ella through, but a part of me just wants it all to stop."

Mav shuffles closer. "Maybe we could negotiate terms with his solicitor? Push for a job transfer."

I look at him to see if he's serious. "Can we do that?"

"He might refuse to, but we can try. A judge might grant a prevention order to keep him away from you and Ella. I'll have Lock get a mobile phone for you. You can call Neve in the morning and talk it over with her."

I smile, leaning into him and resting my head on his broad shoulder. "Thank you," I whisper.

"Rosey moved away," he mutters. I remain still, hardly daring to breathe in case he stops talking. "She had a horrible time at the club. I got her some cash together, and she left. Not long after, I did too. I hit the road to be away from the club and all the toxic shit surrounding it."

"Do you ever hear from her?"

"No. She needed a fresh start, not reminders."

"I'm sorry she left you," I mutter.

"She was the first girl I ever loved. I hadn't even kissed her properly, but I knew I loved her. After," he pauses, "things got bad, I couldn't take it to the next level. I couldn't get it out of my head and move on. I think that hurt her more than the actual bad shit."

"Is that why you hate Crow so much?"

He nods. "When Mum told me she was having a boy, even though I knew it wasn't my dad's kid, I was still secretly excited. I was ten, but the thought of having a kid brother made me happy. I thought Dad would eventually come around and we could all hang out. I imagined showing Crow all the things I'd learnt. But Dad didn't come around. He wouldn't go near him when he was a baby, only to sneer at how much he looked like his real father. So, I did the same. I sneered and rolled my eyes whenever he wanted to play. He eventually got the message. As we got older, Dad played us off against each other, and it's been like that since."

I chew on my lower lip, sad for the brotherhood that was lost between them. "Did Crow claim Rosey?"

"No. Dad wanted some entertainment. He liked the guys to bare--knuckle box against one another. He was bored one night and made Crow and me get in the ring. He knew I wasn't down for it. I was gonna let Crow win just to shut him up, but he brought Rosey into it, offered her up as a prize."

I sit up to look at him better. "How could he do that?"

"She was a whore's daughter, so all bets were kinda off. Rosey was expected to be like her mum and pay her way around the club. I couldn't let Crow win. I knocked him clean out and walked away. I went on a drinking binge with Grim, and when I returned, she was really upset. I thought it was cos I had left her. I tried to tell her that I wasn't gonna fuck her just cos my dad ordered me to. I liked her and I wanted it to be special for her. Anyway, turns out Crow claimed the prize on the grounds I walked out before he was counted out. He forced Rosey to have sex with him. He didn't hold her down as such but made her think she'd be out on the streets along with her mum."

"Oh, Mav, that's awful."

"The worst part of it all, my dad and Ripper were there. They watched that shit happen. It was her first time, Ry. They laughed and touched her up while my twenty-year-old brother fucked her. And every time I think about it, I wanna rip his heart out."

I run my hands over my face. My heart breaks for that poor girl. "No wonder you didn't want me left alone with Crow." I think back to Meli and Ripper, and it's on the tip of my tongue to blurt it all out, but I know it'll break him. "Don't you ever think about contacting her and checking in?"

He shakes his head. "I hurt her by rejecting her. She felt dirty and used, and I made it worse, but I couldn't claim her after that. If I hadn't left her that night, it wouldn't have happened. The guilt's crippling."

I throw my leg over his lap and wrap my arms around his neck, squeezing him tight. "You're such a kind man, Mav. I don't know what I did to deserve you." I kiss him before resting my forehead against his. "On my wedding day, I knew I shouldn't marry Grant. I think that's why he suggested going to Greece to marry so I couldn't run away. Anyway, we stayed in this crappy little bed and breakfast place. We got dressed together, in the same room. There was none of that 'don't see the bride before the big day' bullshit.

"He held me down and raped me while I was wearing my wedding dress. He apologised after, said it was the sight of me looking so pure and beautiful, but I refused to leave the room. I told him I wasn't gonna marry him and I was sick of his behaviour. He locked the door, pushed the wardrobe against it, and locked the windows."

I take a breath, then continue. "He turned on the gas fire. He didn't light it or anything, just let the gas run out into the room. The place was so outdated—who even uses gas fires in Greece? I was worried because the fire was really old-looking and I wasn't convinced it had safety checks or anything like that.

"Anyway, he held a lighter in his hands and told me we were gonna die together. He said he came to Greece to be with me, and if that meant we were on this earth or not, it didn't matter. He laughed while I begged and cried. I was on my knees, trying to convince him we were gonna be fine and I was overthinking what he did. I told him I enjoyed it."

A sob escapes me, and Mav's eyes are filled with pain. He wipes my tears using the pads of his thumbs. "An hour later, we were married and back in that same room like nothing happened. He raped me repeatedly that night because he knew I feared death over a life with him. He had all the control. He used that same threat many times after Ella. She'd cling to me crying, not really understanding what it meant if he was to light that match, but sensing it was bad. Sometimes, when things were really bad, I'd silently pray for him to do it. Because at least we'd be free."

"Fuck, baby. You'll never go through that again. I'll keep you and Ella safe forever."

CHAPTER SEVENTEEN

MAVERICK

Since my confession to Rylee two nights ago, things have been good between us. Then her opening up like that just made our connection stronger. I can't keep my hands off her, and I'm wrapped around her at every chance I get. She called Neve and put her proposal forward. We're waiting to hear if Grant agrees, but we haven't let it weigh on us.

Since Ella wasn't registered at birth, Meli has organised a party. Earlier today, I took Rylee and Ella to the registry office, where Neve had arranged for her to be registered. She left Grant off the birth certificate because apparently, unless you're married, both parties have to be present. Rylee was pleased. We followed it up with ice cream at the park so Meli could make the arrangements back at the club. When we enter the clubhouse and everyone is gathered with balloons and banners, Ella claps in delight. She's swept off in my mum's arms towards a huge cake in the centre of the room, and Rylee kisses me. "Did you do this?"

"All Meli," I explain, and she goes off to find her.

Grim joins me. "You heard from Carter's solicitor?" I shake my head. "If he accepts that bullshit proposal, tell me you're not leaving it like that?"

I smirk. "Do you know me at all? There's no way that piece of shit is riding off into the sunset with his pregnant girlfriend so he can do the same to her. I'm not stupid—he'll never leave Rylee alone. He'll pay my way."

Grim slaps me on the back. "Good, man, cos the brothers love Rylee, and they want that motherfucker to pay for what he did to her and Ella."

The Taylors arrive and we shake hands. The sale of our land is going through, and the guys are coming up with great investment ideas, some I'd like Arthur's advice on. As I go to my office to get the details on some of the properties we like, I spot Meli and Ripper talking in the corner. He looks mad as hell, and I don't like the way he's waving his arms around. "Things alright over here?" I ask, taking them both by surprise.

Meli stays quiet, which is unusual. "I caught her sneaking out," says Ripper.

I take in Meli's outfit of shorts and a vest. "You were going out like that?" I query. "Where to?"

"It don't matter, Pres. I sorted it," says Ripper. He stares at me like he's expecting me to leave it, but something doesn't feel right.

"Meli, Rylee is looking for you. Go find her." She doesn't need telling twice and slips under Ripper's arm where he rests it against the wall.

"What's going on?" I ask.

"I told you, she was gonna sneak out."

"Meli never leaves dressed like that, not even for shopping. She's been excited for this party all day, so why would she leave something she arranged?"

Ripper shrugs. "I don't know, Pres. Maybe she planned this to distract us from her going out."

"I don't like the way she looked scared just then. I don't know what's going on, but I will find out, brother, you can trust me on that. In the meantime, I'm putting Grim back on her. You can go back on the debt collections for Arthur." He starts to walk away, and I grab him by the arm. "Ripper, if I find out you're seeing my sister, things will get ugly real fast." The thought of one of our eldest members fucking my sister makes me shudder with repulsion. Surely, he isn't Meli's type?

When I go back to the party, Meli is whispering in the corner with Rylee and Hadley. I'll ask Rylee about it later, but right now, I have business to deal with.

Arthur looks over the listings and points out a few details I should watch out for. I know most of his businesses are a cover for the underground shit he does, but he knows his stuff and we only have one shot to get this right so we can pull the club into this century and get the cash rolling in.

A call comes in from Neve. "Sorry to bother you. I know you're celebrating Ella today, but I just wanted to let you know Carter agreed to the terms." I nod to Grim, who's staring at me, waiting for confirmation. "The judge will grant a prevention order for Rylee and Ella, and that will be for three years. It'll be reviewed after that. They didn't want to disclose an exact location, but it's somewhere in Ireland, so she's not going to bump into him accidentally. Just don't go booking your holidays there."

"And it's on his record?" I ask.

"There's a marker. It's not instantly retrievable unless a top cop looks into it, but it's there. I know this is what Rylee wanted, but I can't help thinking this is a mistake."

"I totally agree with you, Neve, but she can't face the idea of standing up in court and being in the same room as him. She's just not ready for that."

I hang up and fill Grim in. "No leaving date?" he asks. I shake my head.

"I'll put a guy on him, and we'll target him the day he leaves. No one will miss him then. By the way, you're back on Meli duty," I tell him.

He groans. "Ah, fuck. Just let her do her thing. We're not gonna catch Eagle's killer and no one else has been targeted. We can't keep her inside forever."

"First of all, it was your idea to keep an eye on her. And secondly, something's not right there. I want you to keep a close eye on her. Try and make friends and see if she talks to you."

"She won't talk to me," he says, laughing. "What's her problem?"

I shrug. "I don't know. I caught Ripper leaning right in on her, and it looked serious. He was pissed about something but made some bullshit excuse about her sneaking out."

"Dressed like that?"

"That's what I said. You don't think they're together, do yah?"

Grim almost spits his beer out and his eyes narrow. "He's old enough to be her dad!"

"That's what worries me."

"I'll talk to Hadley. She'll know."

"Maybe I've got it wrong, but something isn't sitting right."

"What's wrong with Meli?" asks Arthur, stepping closer.

"Not sure." I shrug. "You know what siblings are like. Pain in the arse," I say, and he nods, staring at Meli dancing with Ella in her arms.

"Arthur can always help her out if she's going off the rails." Tommy grins, rubbing Arthur's shoulder. "You love a challenge, don't you, brother."

"We've got it covered," snaps Grim. "Thanks, though." I eye him, wondering what's up his arse. "I'm gonna check in with Hadley." He stalks off.

"A touch of the green-eyed monster there," Tommy says.

I frown. "I don't think so. He hates Meli."

Tommy sniggers. "Man, if that was hate, I'll walk on broken glass."

In the evening, Rylee takes Ella off to bed and I follow her. I wait in the bedroom, and the second she steps through the door, I pull her to me and kiss her. She laughs, smacking my shoulders. "It's only been a day. You need to control yourself."

"You're too irresistible," I mumble into her neck.

"I promised Meli I'd have a drink with her," she says, pulling away.

"Do you know what's going on between her and Ripper?"

She pauses and looks flustered for a minute. "Ripper?"

"Yeah, you know, that big, ugly bastard who's been in this club since the beginning."

She turns to the mirror and fusses with her hair. "No. No . . . erm . . . I don't have a clue."

I go behind her and wrap my arms around her waist. "I'd believe that, Bandia, if you knew how to lie. It's written all over your face. What's going on?"

She turns to face me with sadness in her eyes. "Mav, I can't tell you. It's her story, and she really, really doesn't want me to tell you."

"See, now you got me worried. Are they a thing?"

She shakes her head, and I feel slightly relieved. "No. Look, I think Meli will tell you eventually, but be patient."

What choice do I have? I hope Grim has more luck with Hadley.

RYLEE

Sometimes, I want to ask Grant questions. I often lie here, when I'm alone, and think of the many answers I don't have. Like why the fuck didn't he register our daughter's birth? I remember the day clearly—Ella was only a week old, and I was battered and bruised, so Grant said he'd go and register her for me. I thought he was doing a nice thing, like he was making up for hurting me. He told me they'd send the birth certificate in the mail, only I wasn't allowed to open mail, not that anything ever came for me. I guess I was so busy looking after Ella and trying to keep on his good side, I never followed it up.

Hadley joins myself and Meli on the couch. "Grim is on to us," she whispers, trying not to move her lips.

"Yeah, so is Mav," I add.

"Oh shit," mutters Meli.

"So, we need to come up with a convincing lie quickly," says Hadley.

"Ripper is so mad I told you guys."

He'd had a real go at her tonight after she confessed to telling us. She won't say why it came up in conversation, but I can't imagine she told him for no reason. And now Maverick's witnessed their argument, he's suspicious. If it was up to me, I'd tell him. He'll get rid of the scumbag and Meli could be happy again, but she's terrified of any of the guys finding out.

"Mav's just told me Grant accepted the deal. He's moving away to Ireland," I say, and the girls smile.

"That's great, Rylee. You'll be able to relax knowing he's gone," says Hadley.

Meli presses her lips together before sighing. "Do you think he'll go?" she asks, and I stare at her blankly.

"Assuming his boss will make sure of it, yes."

"And if he doesn't? I don't mean to be the bearer of shit news, but he is kinda obsessed, and I'm worried he won't leave."

"He still can't come near us. The judge granted an injunction."

Meli shrugs, not looking convinced, and her worry weighs heavy on my mind.

∞

Maverick plants kisses along my neck and over my chest. He stops when I don't respond, and I smile awkwardly. "I'm trying to woo you here, the least you could do is look more into it."

I grin. "Sorry. I'm thinking of Grant." The moment the words leave my lips, I regret them. Maverick rolls to my side, covering his face behind his arm. "Oh god . . . I didn't mean like that." I rush to make it right, nuzzling into him. He flinches away, and I wince. "Mav, I didn't mean that. Meli said something earlier and it's playing on my mind."

"Meli strikes again," he mutters.

"What if he doesn't leave?"

"He will."

"I want to be confident like you, but it's niggling at me."

He turns on his side and props himself up on the pillows. "Bandia, Grant is moving to Ireland. I promise. I'll personally make sure of it."

I narrow my eyes, and he looks away. "I don't want you anywhere near him. Don't do anything stupid."

"Please," he says easily, "as if."

"Maverick, I'm serious." I sit up. "You agreed to let me deal with this, and I have."

"And I've let you."

"You haven't *let* me. I didn't need your permission."

He groans and throws his leg over me, pulling me to lie down. "I just meant I'll check his boat ticket or plane or however the fuck he plans on getting there. I'll have a guy watch him leave. That way, we know he's gone."

I relax a little and nod. "Right, well, I guess that's okay."

"You wanna tell me about Meli yet?" he adds.

I pull him in for a kiss, taking his mind off all things Meli and Ripper.

∞

We spend the following day taking Ella to different nurseries to get a feel for them. Now we have a birth certificate, there's no stopping us. Mav insists on carrying Ella most of the time, and as much as I encourage her to walk, it makes my heart melt when I see him bouncing her up and down as he entertains her with pony rides.

One of the nurseries take us into the office to discuss routines, and when they refer to Mav as 'Dad', he doesn't correct them. I know it's too soon to be talking love, but I'm seriously heading that way, and I'm pretty sure he is too, but he's scared to say it because he doesn't want to rush me.

We're walking along the corridor in the next place, hand-in-hand, with the headteacher chatting away about the artworks displayed on the wall, when I squeeze Mav's hand. He glances at me, and I smile. "I love you," I mouth. I must hold my breath for a full twenty seconds before he stops dead, grabs my chin in one hand, and tugs me to kiss him. The headteacher stops too to see what's happening, and I blush.

"Bandia, I fucking love you so much."

"Oh, I say," mutters the headteacher, and I laugh. I love that he doesn't change for anything or anyone. He is who he is, curse words and all.

"So, I told Mav I love him," I say to Nelly, and her eyes widen in delight.

"I take it he said it back?"

"He did." I grin wider. "I can't believe how lucky I am. Who walks out of that sort of situation and lands on their feet like this?"

"Can I just remind you it's all down to me," she says, laughing.

"But seriously, thank you. I know I've said it a million times, but I'm so grateful. You saved my life. And if there's any way I can repay you, just say the words."

She sips her cocktail. "Um, maybe you could find me a hot ass man."

"We have a whole club, take your pick."

She grins. "I'm kidding. I like being single. No drama."

Mav rushes over. "Bandia, I gotta go. I'll call you at some point, but it might be an all-nighter. I love you." He kisses me on the head.

"I love you too," I reply and watch his retreating back as he and Grim rush off.

"That was so cute." Nelly grins. "You lucky bitch."

CHAPTER EIGHTEEN

MAVERICK

Carter isn't stupid. He booked a train ticket, a coach, and a ferry, all at different times. My men have been to every one and he hasn't appeared. But getting a call from Ghost to say he'd spotted him leaving his home with a duffel bag, dressed in black and wearing a baseball cap, rang alarm bells. Ghost followed him to the docks while we were en route, and as we pull up on our bikes, he's waiting impatiently.

"He's checked in to get on the next ferry," he explains.

"Where is he now?"

"He's by the water, yelling into his mobile."

I smile at Grim. "Excellent. Let's go."

I spot him the second we round the corner. He's just finished his call and he appears agitated. He throws his mobile into the water and it splashes with a plop in the silence. "Temper, temper," says Grim, and Carter spins to face us. It's dark, but I swear I see his face pale. He glances around nervously, but it's no use, there's no one around, which is why he came around here to use his mobile. There was no one to listen in.

"Fancy seeing you here," I say. "Going anywhere nice?"

"You can't fucking touch me. They'll know it's you if I go missing!"

"I'm not used to seeing this side of you, Grant." Grim smirks. "I have to say, it's very disappointing. I hate a weak man."

"I'm doing what she fucking asked," he spits out through gritted teeth.

"But for how long?" I ask. "You're not leaving her forever, and I can't take the chance you might return one day and turn her life upside down."

"Why didn't you register your daughter's birth? Were you planning on doing something to her?" asks Grim.

"Don't be fucking stupid."

"Why else wouldn't you want any trace of a person?" Grim snaps.

"I didn't want Rylee doing anything stupid, like trying to get her a passport," he admits. "I wasn't gonna hurt Ella—I just didn't want them to leave."

A text comes through from Arthur to say our boat is ready. I smile at Grim, and he pulls out his gun. "We're going on a little journey, to make sure you're definitely leaving."

"I am," he hisses, panic in his tone. "I've booked the ferry."

"No need for that. We'll take you first class." I grab his hands and cuff him behind his back. Grim keeps the gun pointed at him as we move further along the docks towards a row of containers. Behind them, bobbing up and down in the water is a speedboat. Carter tenses, trying to dig his feet in the dirt to stop me pushing him forward. It doesn't work.

A man steps from the boat and hands the keys to Grim. We shake hands before he disappears, then Ghost steps aboard. "Welcome aboard. Please keep your hands in the boat at all times and try not to fall overboard," he says, winking as we also step onto the boat.

Ghost starts the engine. "Please," mutters Carter, and I roll my eyes. I wonder how many times he made Rylee beg for her life. We speed through the dark, murky water. It's fucking cold out here, and Carter begins to shake. "I'm sorry for what I did. I just loved her so fucking much—" I shoot my hand out and grip his neck, squeezing hard until he's gasping.

"Fuck you, you piece of shit. You didn't love her. What you did wasn't out of love. Did you know she kept a diary?" I sneer as his eyes begin to water. "I read some of it, and yah know what, it made me sick to my stomach. Rape, daily beatings, general bullying. You fucking put her outside naked after she gave birth to your daughter! You left her out there in the rain and made her watch you eat the fucking dinner she cooked you!" I shake his body before shoving him hard away from me. He lands on his side, coughing violently. "You honestly thought I'd let you walk away?"

"I've got a new life," he splutters. "A kid on the way."

I laugh. "You don't deserve it."

"That's not up to you. You're not the decider on people's lives. I fucked up, but you can't decide my fate."

Grim laughs. "Because we should trust in the law, right?"

"There's a process," he mutters.

I land my boot on his shin, the bone cracks, and he cries out. "Fuck the process. Fuck you. Fuck the law. You won't get a chance to mess up anyone else's life ever again."

I grab some rope and bind his ankles together. He sobs from the pain as I pull his legs together. I punch him in the ribs, making sure to break a few of them too. He needs to feel a fraction of the pain he caused my ol' lady. "I never understand what you get out of the shit you do," I begin, tying the ropes tightly and then dragging a weight over and attaching the rope to that. "Is it a power trip? Do you get fucking hard with each punch? What is it about having a crying woman at your mercy that makes you do the shit you do?"

"Please," he begs, "don't do this. Rylee will never forgive you." I punch him in the face. How dare he claim to know what she'll forgive?

"And I get to wondering how many vulnerable people you've been called out to as a cop and have hurt?" His expression changes, and I know without doubt I've hit the nail on the head. "We're doing the world a favour," I add. "I'm gonna take care of Rylee, and I want you to have that image on your brain as you suck in your last breath of dirty water—me and Rylee and my little girl, Ella, living happily ever after. And you, well," I look out to the water, "you'll rot amongst the dirt at the bottom of the sea where you belong." I nod to Grim, and we each grab a part of Carter.

"Wait, wait, wait," he panics.

"Rest in hell, motherfucker," I mutter before shoving him over the side of the boat. There's a large splash and we watch over the edge as his body is pulled down by the weight. Bubbles surface and I take a seat, watching them pop.

"Rylee can never know about this," I mutter. Grim and Ghost nod. "We say we watched him get on the ferry and we left."

∞

The following day, I force myself to smile and act normal. I don't feel guilty for what I did cos Carter deserved to die, but I hate keeping the truth from Rylee. I call church and fill the men in. There's relief around the table. "He needed to pay," mutters Copper.

"And we like having her around, Pres," says Ghost. "We can't cope without her cooking skills," he adds as a joke.

I smile. "That brings me to the next thing. I want to claim her, officially. I haven't talked to her about it yet, but we're heading in that direction."

Cheers erupt and hands reach out for me to shake. "Congrats, Pres." Copper is the first to shake my hand and slap me on the back, followed by everyone else. Everyone except for Crow, who remains seated.

"You not happy for our President?" asks Grim.

"Should I be?" he asks.

"Damn straight you should be," snaps Ghost. "This club is going in the right direction, finally."

He sneers, shaking his head. "Rylee might not wanna be your ol' lady. You ever thought of that?"

"Then I'll wait until she's ready," I say.

"What if she wants another brother?"

I ball my fists. "She won't."

"Rosey did," he says. I can't hold the rage in as I land my first punch on his jaw. Grim orders the guys to step back. This fight's been coming for too long, and Crow needs put in his place. He shoves me away from him, landing a punch to my face. I shake it off and grab him by the collar, slamming him against the wall.

"You fucking disgust me," I spit. "Rosey hated you."

"She fucking loved it, man. I still hear her cries of ecstasy."

"You're deluded. You made her skin crawl. It was no better than rape!"

He growls, shoving me from him. I fall back, stumbling out the open door and into

the main room. Crow rushes me, rugby tackling me into the nearest wall and throwing some punches against my abdomen. I manage to get him off and slam my fist into his face, busting his nose and spraying us both in blood.

"Stop!" I hear Mum yelling from somewhere in the room, and I catch Grim pulling her away. Rylee is with them, her face full of worry.

"I'm so sick of you looking at me like what I did was wrong," he growls, hitting me back and splitting my eyebrow. I feel the blood trickling down my cheek.

"It was wrong! You know it was!"

"What choice did I have?" he yells, shoving me in the chest. "I was twenty and I had to impress that fucking bastard because I was never enough. Whatever I did, it was never enough!"

"None of us were enough, Crow. It was his issue, not ours." We stare at each other, our chests heaving. "He wanted this," I add. "He wanted you to think you were not enough, but you are . . . we all are!"

He looks lost for a second before sighing. "It haunts me. Rosey," he admits.

"Shit like that does."

"Show's over, brothers. Get on with your day," orders Grim and the brothers disperse. "Go sort this shit out in the office," he adds. I head to it and relax when I hear Crow behind me. It's time to put this shit to bed once and for all.

I hand him a tissue for his nose and grab another to mop the blood from my brow. "He'd have loved that," I say.

"He got off on violence," adds Crow.

"I never set out to hate you. He made it impossible to bond with you cos I was a stupid kid who thought the sun shone out his arse. I wanted to impress him."

"Same."

"But when I stepped away, I realised how toxic it was. He evoked bad feelings all around this place. I used to lie on the floor outside his bedroom, listening to him beat Mum and spit his venomous words at her. I didn't want to get on that wrong side of him, so I went above and beyond to show how loyal I was."

Crow smirks. "But it didn't matter. I did the same and it still wasn't good enough."

"I thought if I stepped away, he'd accept you more. He made you his VP."

"He just wanted to make me do his dirty shit. He had me beating innocent people while he smashed up their businesses, just because they couldn't afford his ridiculous protection prices. Shit, they didn't need protection from anyone but him."

"That's why I want to make shit better around here, Crow. I don't wanna end up like him."

"Talking to Rylee made me see," he begins, "what it feels like to love." I freeze, and his eyes meet mine. "Don't panic, I know she's yours. But I couldn't help it. She's got this light around her that shines through to even the darkest heart. She's a good woman, brother. Look after her."

"You not gonna stick around?" I ask, frowning.

He shakes his head. "I can't. We're not gonna work. Too much has happened."

I nod in agreement. "There will always be a place here for you, Crow. When you're ready."

∞

I find Rylee outside, sitting on the grass with her knees hugged to her chest and staring out across the field in a daydream. "I'm sorry," I say from behind her, and she glances back over her shoulder. "That was a shitshow of how brothers deal with years of emotional abuse."

"Is he okay?" she asks as I take a seat beside her. "Are you?" she adds.

"Nothing we can't fix with a few drinks and a game of football."

"I hated seeing you like that," she whispers, and I place my arm around her shoulders. "It's not the man I know."

Shoving Carter from the boat flashes through my mind. "You have to separate the man I am with you from the club president. I have expectations to meet, and if a brother shows that sort of disrespect, he's gonna get a beating."

"If you're gonna house women here who have escaped such violence, you have to control that side of things. Women like me have spent years with the fight or flight sense, and you don't know what that sets off in a person when violence erupts like that out of nowhere."

I kiss her gently on the side of her head. "I'm sorry, Bandia, I didn't think. Now we've got it out of our systems, things will be better. Besides, Crow's leaving the club for a while."

She scowls at me. "What?"

"Don't look so upset," I mutter in annoyance.

"Have you kicked him out?"

"No. His choice, not mine, but I think it's for the best."

She pushes to her feet. "I don't. He needs to be around. Hadley and Meli need him here."

I also stand. "Why are you so bothered about Crow?"

"He's not as bad as you think," she snaps. "He needs family around him."

"Or a good woman, right?" I snap.

She narrows her eyes. "What's that supposed to mean?"

"It means, if you like him, Rylee, just tell me. Don't fucking lead me on and leave me for that shit."

She stares up at me and a range of emotions pass over her face. "I told you I love you."

"My mum told my dad that every damn day, didn't stop her fucking his VP." Hurt passes over Rylee's face and I inwardly groan. I'm fucking this up. I know she doesn't like Crow in that way, but with his confession weighing fresh in my mind and her reluctance to let him go . . . "Go fucking beg him to stay, Rylee. Don't let me stop you." I stomp off in the direction of the trees, putting some much-needed distance between us.

RYLEE

I sit on Crow's bed, watching him shove clothes haphazardly into a duffel. I laugh at his terrible attempt to fold a shirt and take it from him. "Where will you go?"

"No real plans," he mutters. "Just gonna see where the road takes me."

"I wish you'd stay. There's gonna be so many women who'll need help, and you're a great listener."

"Well, I wasn't always this way," he says.

"I know." I smile when he gives me a quizzical look. I sigh, grabbing another shirt and folding it. "I know about Rosey." He looks annoyed, so I rush to add, "I'm not judging. I just know a lot happened back then and I don't think you or Maverick were to blame for any of it. Your dad was an adult, he shouldn't have encouraged any of it."

"That's what MC life is all about, Rylee—violence, sex, drugs, and crime."

I smile. "You don't believe that, Crow. Stick around and give Mav a chance to prove that."

He scoffs. "You really believe in him, don't you?" I nod. "You know, he first killed a man when he was ten years old. It was like a rite of passage back then. He needed to show the men he had a leader's blood. He took out my father with a bullet to the head and didn't flinch. I wasn't there," he says, stuffing the folded shirts into his bag, "but the men still talk about it to this day. They say he has the devil inside of him, you just gotta poke him hard enough to see it."

"That was in the past, just like you and Rosey. Your dad orchestrated it all."

He shakes his head. "Don't kid yourself. Would Ella shoot a man and not cry? It isn't normal to look someone in the eye, kill them, and walk away without a shred of remorse, not at that age."

"I don't know what you're trying to do," I mutter, "but he's a good man now and that's all that matters."

"A good man," he repeats, shaking his head like it's the funniest thing he's ever heard. "Would a good man kill your ex?" I gasp, my hands flying to my open mouth, and I shake my head. He wouldn't kill Grant. He promised he'd let me sort it my way. "He took your man prisoner, forced him into a boat at the docks, took him out into the deepest depths of the water, beat him, tied him to a weight, and pushed him overboard to drown. Is that a good man, Rylee?"

"He wouldn't," I whisper, wanting desperately to believe it.

"Call him," says Crow. "Call Grant. If he's alive, he'd pick up, right, especially for you?" He holds out his mobile, and I take it with shaky hands. Dialling Grant's number carefully, I stare at Crow as I press the phone to my ear and wait for him to answer. Only he doesn't and it goes straight to voicemail. Crow takes me by the hand. "Listen, I can take you away from this. I can get you and Ella a fresh start away from them all."

My mind races and I can't think straight. That's where Maverick disappeared to last night. It's why he had to rush off so suddenly. Sickness bubbles in my stomach and I rub the area like that'll somehow ease the pain in my chest. I hate Grant with everything I have, but knowing he died like that, suffocating on the water . . . a sob escapes me, and Crow wraps me in his arms. "Let's get Ella and get out of here."

I shake my head. "No, I have nowhere to go."

"I'll find you somewhere. I can't leave you here. He's just as evil as his dad. That won't change because he smiles and pretends he cares about you." He's already leading me from the room and heading downstairs with his hand pressing on the small of my back.

I take Ella by the hand. There's hardly anyone around, just Brea. "Just going for a drive, Mum," says Crow, and she nods, not taking her eyes from the television.

We get outside, and I stop. "It's going to be okay," he reassures me.

But I can't leave. Not without speaking to Mav first. "I need to hear it from him."

"He'll talk his way out of it." Crow shoves me a little harder towards the exit.

"Everything okay, brother?" asks Ripper, stepping from the shadows. I hate the way he sneers at me, especially now he knows I'm aware of his secret.

"I'm having trouble getting Rylee to believe me that this place is not good for her. She needs to leave with me, today."

Ripper raises his eyebrows. "Brother's right. Get out of here while you can."

"I don't want to leave," I say, frowning.

Ripper throws a set of keys at Crow. "Take my van. I'll help you get her in the back."

I start to back away, but Crow grabs me by the wrist. "Stop," I hiss. Ella begins to cry, and Ripper scoops her up in his arms, turning my blood cold. "Put her down," I growl.

He grins. "I'm just helping out a brother."

I don't think. I clear my mind, just how Grim told me, and I raise my knee hard and fast, connecting with Ripper's crotch. He groans, lowering to the ground and releasing Ella, who runs to me. "You fucking bitch," he hisses.

I swing around, slapping Crow hard. It takes him by surprise, and I use those few seconds to push my thumbs into his eyes. He cries out, dropping to his knees.

"Jesus, I feel like playing an empowering song." The female voice surprises me but also floods me with relief, until I turn to find a woman I've never seen before, holding a gun.

She pulls out her mobile phone. "I have the perfect one," she says, sounding excited. I eye the gun cautiously, though she isn't pointing it at me. It hangs by her side as she presses something on her mobile and music begins to play. "It's this part," she says, grinning. "Credit where it's due cos you don't like pussy in power . . . Venom." She laughs, pausing the music. "Little Simz, 'Venom'," she explains.

Ripper tries to stand, but she aims the gun at him. "I wouldn't bother, Ripper. I don't want to kill you in front of the little one."

"Rosey?" he croaks.

"Not how you remember me, right?" she asks, still smiling like it's the most normal thing in the world to be waving a gun around. "What do you think of the hair?" She flicks her black locks with the gun, and I flinch. "I wasn't sold at first, but I like to hide in the shadows and red hair doesn't make you inconspicuous. Besides, I think it makes my blue eyes stand out." She leans forward as if to show me her eyes, blinking a few times. I nod slowly because I think she's waiting for me to agree.

Rosey crouches down before Ella and hands her a lollipop. "You are the cutest little button I ever saw. I want you to do me a really big favour." Ella glances at me, and I nod, forcing a smile to reassure her.

"Can you go back inside and watch television with Brea? But you can't tell her I'm out here. It's a big surprise." Ella nods. "Good girl." We wait in silence for Ella to disappear inside. "You were wise to get his hands off your little girl," says Rosey. "Ripper likes to touch up little girls, don't you, brother?" She spits the words, and he hangs his head. "I promised Amelia I'd be back one day and I'd make you pay for what you did to her."

Crow fidgets on his knees, bringing her attention to him. "And then there's you," she whispers, and for a second, I see pain in her eyes. "You know what I see when I close my eyes, Crow?" He shakes his head. "I see you, leering down at me as you take my virginity."

"It haunts me too," he mutters. "I hate myself."

She laughs, pushing the gun to his forehead and forcing him to look up into her eyes. "I hate you more." She pulls the trigger, and I jump back, screaming in shock as his head explodes and his body slumps to the ground.

CHAPTER NINETEEN

MAVERICK

A gunshot rings out and I take off in the direction of the club. By the time I reach the entrance, my lungs burn in my chest and I gasp for breath, halting at the scene before me. I have my gun in my hand, but I don't raise it because I'm too lost in her blue eyes, the ones I once knew so well. "Aww, the hero himself," says Rosey with a cruel smile. "You were almost too late again, boo," she says in a mocking voice, tipping her head to the side and giving me a sympathetic smile. "He's good at showing up late," she adds to Rylee. Rylee . . . I didn't see her. She looks terrified, with her eyes wide and her hands covering her mouth. "Tell her, Mav. Tell her how you always barge in after the event. You'd never make a superhero. You don't see Spiderman showing up late."

"Rosey," I mutter, putting my gun away and holding out my hands in a placating manner. "What are you doing?"

"I'm here to set things right," she says, smiling maniacally.

"This isn't like you, baby. Talk to me."

She laughs wildly, throwing her head back. "Talk? You want to talk now?"

"I want to understand."

She rubs the gun along her lower lip like she's thinking about it. "I don't need your understanding now. It's too late."

"You know, if I could change all that shit, I would."

"Tell me, Mav, what brought you back here?"

"Eagle died," I say bluntly, and she grins, biting on her lower lip. "I came back to run this place."

"I know. I've been watching you."

"Why?"

"Because when your dad died, I wanted to make sure that piece of shit didn't take over," she snaps, pointing the gun in Crow's direction. Blood surrounds him, and I glance around nervously, hoping no one passing by sees the fucking mess. "Do you know why your dad was in that back alley?" Rosey asks, bringing my attention back to her, and I shake my head. "He was paying me money to keep quiet."

"About?"

"Your brother," she says as she hops from one foot to the other like she's excited to tell the secret. "You see, your dad decided he liked what he saw after Crow fucked me. So, he took his turn. As did Ripper. And then you sent me away, and I didn't get a chance to tell anyone about the seed one of them planted in my belly." My mouth falls open. "Of course, he demanded DNA, and guess what, your daddy had a fourth child."

"Fuck," I mutter. "Why didn't you find me?"

"And say what? You were already disgusted with me, you could hardly look at me."

"I wasn't," I growl. "I was mad at myself for letting you down. I should have been here."

"It's water under the bridge," she sing-songs. "These days, I don't need a man to rely on. I take out a dozen of these bastards a day."

"You kill people?" I ask.

"I get paid to rid the world of rubbish," she says happily. "I have the best job." She sighs, crouching down in front of Ripper. "Which brings me to this piece of shit." Ripper spits at her feet, and she hits him hard with the butt of the gun.

"Rosey, I can't let you kill any more of my men."

She makes eye contact. "Then stop me, Mav." I draw my gun again, and she smirks. "Would you still feel the same if I was to tell you Ripper's secret?"

"Tell me and let the club deal with him. I don't want any more bodies piled up out here."

"I can't let you do that, Pres," she says, smiling again. "I owe Meli this one."

"Meli?" I repeat, confused.

"Your dad knew, of course. But then, he wasn't quite the morally caring kind of man himself. I was only twenty-one, but Meli, she was much younger when it started. Wasn't she, Ripper?" My blood runs cold and I grip the gun tighter. My palms sweat and my breathing speeds up. "No, Meli was just a little kid. Not even a teenager before you forced yourself on her, ripping her virginity from her and using her twin sister as a threat to keep returning."

"No," I growl.

"Yep," says Rosey. "And your dad found out. Now, he did the right thing, he threatened Ripper to leave his kids alone, but that's all he did. He didn't make him pay. Poor Meli suffered for years, and all daddy dearest did was blame her. He said she provoked Ripper with her slutty dress sense."

"Brother," I hiss, "say something." He raises his head to look me in the eye, and I see it. I see the guilt and the disgust right there. "No!" I yell as I squeeze the trigger, hitting him in the right eye. He falls to the ground with a heavy thud. My ears ring from the sound of the gun going off, and as the ringing clears, I hear Rylee screaming. I tuck my gun away and rush to her, dragging her into my chest and hushing her. I watch as Rosey stands, wiping blood splatter from her face using her sleeve, but it just smudges it further.

"That was my shot," she says, looking pissed off. "Now was not the time to play hero."

"I got caught up in the moment," I mutter, rubbing gentle circles on Rylee's back as she sobs against me.

Grim drives through the gate, jumping off his bike the second he stops. "What the fuck?"

Rosey rushes to Grim and throws herself into his arms. He looks confused as she hugs him. "It's me, Rosey."

"I recognised you," he says dryly. "It's the rest that got me confused."

"Grim, take Rylee inside. I've gotta clean this mess up." Rylee shakes her head, but I push her into Grim's arms, and he leads her away as I put a call in to Arthur.

"Mav?" he greets.

"Arthur, have you filled in the foundations of your new club yet?" I ask.

"No," he pauses. "Fuck, Mav, don't you think there's enough skeletons down there already?"

"It was unexpected."

He sighs. "You want me to arrange clean-up?"

"Please. It's outside the clubhouse."

Rosey watches me move some empty oil drums in front of both bodies to hide them from public view. "What the fuck were you thinking turning up here in the middle of the day?"

"It wasn't the plan," she says, shrugging, "but your men were taking that chick without her permission, so I had to intervene."

"They were taking Rylee?"

She nods. "She put up a good fight, but it wouldn't have done her any good. They were set on her leaving with Crow today."

"I better go and check on her," I mutter, heading for the door. I hear Rosey's footsteps, and she pulls on my arm to stop me.

"Is it okay if I stick around for a bit? I'd love to catch up." I nod and head inside. I don't know how the fuck to feel, seeing her again like this, and now, two of my brothers are fucking dead. And the secrets . . . *fuck*, the secrets.

Rylee is in my office with Grim. She's taking a sip of whiskey even though her hand is shaking and the contents of the glass are sloshing around. Grim pats me on the shoulder, leaving us alone. "Stupid question, but are you okay?"

She sucks in a deep breath. "I don't know."

"It's a lot to take in. Seeing a dead body for the first time is—"

"Well, you should know, right?" she mutters, staring into her drink.

"What?"

"It's not the first time for you, is it?" She looks at me, her eyes searching my face.

"Well, no, but what does that have to do with any of it?"

She shrugs. "I'm fine if you need to go and catch up with Rosey. I might take Ella for a walk. Maybe get an ice-cream . . ."

I frown as she stands, placing her drink on the desk. "Alone?"

"Yes. It's not like Grant will pop up, is it?" I open my mouth to speak but press it closed again. "He's in Ireland, right?" she asks, and I find myself nodding.

She moves towards the door. "I still think you shouldn't be alone right now, not after everything," I blurt out.

Her hand rests on the door handle and she bows her head before taking another deep breath. "Yah know what, I just need some space. I need to be alone with my daughter to process everything."

"One last thing," I add, and she sighs. "Was that the secret you were hiding for Meli? Ripper hurting her like that?"

Her eyes find mine and they're full of guilt. She nods once, then pulls the door open and marches out. I flop down in my chair and grab her whiskey. Knocking it back, even though I hate the stuff, I gag just as Grim stalks back in. "What the fuck is going on?"

"I don't know where to start," I say, rubbing my brow. "I've got two dead men, accusations flying around, and an ol' lady who fucking hates me right now."

"I've sent the women to their rooms, told them it was for safety, but I don't think your mum was convinced. She knows something is wrong. She asked me to call Crow, said he went out somewhere."

"He did. He just ain't coming back." I slam my fists on the table. "Fuck!"

"I assume she did this for revenge?"

"Yeah. She was behind Dad's death too. She took them all out for what they did to her and half of me doesn't blame her."

"And the other half?"

"Is mad she didn't let me deal with Ripper properly."

"It was in the past. Besides, although he was there, was it worth his life?"

I narrow my eyes. "I took Ripper. It was a snap decision, and I wasn't thinking straight."

He lowers into a chair. "You shot him?"

"I got to the bottom of him and Meli."

Grim sits a little straighter, his full attention on me. "They were together?"

I shake my head. "Worse. He abused her, Grim. For fucking years, he abused my kid sister. And it gets worse," I snap as he balls his fists. "Dad knew about it. He blamed her, said it was her outfits! So now, I'm left with a fuck load of questions and no fucker left to answer them. So yeah, I'm glad Rosey came for those fuckers, but I need closure and there's no chance of that now."

"Piece of fucking shit," he roars, standing and pacing. "How didn't we know?"

"We were too busy looking after ourselves," I mutter bitterly, holding my head in my hands. "I gotta have that conversation with Meli and then I need to tell Mum some things. Rosey has a kid, and Eagle is the father."

Grim freezes, his eyes bugging out of his head. "What the fuck? I go for a ride and come back to a reality show!"

"Tell me about it. I knew the club was a mess, but never in my life did I think evil ran so deep. We gotta hold church right after I've spoken to Meli."

RYLEE

I watch Ella rolling around on the grass at the back of the club. After all the bravado with Mav, I couldn't quite take myself out those gates. I groan out loud. I fucking love him. After everything, I fucking love him. *I'm an idiot.*

"Mind if I join you?" Rosey asks, dropping down beside me. I'm terrified of this crazy woman and I think she senses that because she offers a warm smile. "I'm not so bad."

"I just watched you execute a man before my eyes," I mutter.

"I sent your little girl in before I did it, though," she says with a smile. I think she's actually lost her mind.

"What do you want?" I ask.

"I want to stick around here for a while. Now I've cleaned the place up, I think I'd like to come back."

"And why are you asking me? It's not my decision."

"Are you kidding? You're the new queen around here. All decisions like this come back to you. Mav will pretend they don't, to save his manly ego, but ultimately, it's you who decides if I stay or go."

I frown, shaking my head. "I have no say. I'm just a cook."

"I've been watching this place for months. You're not just a cook, Rylee. You're a fighter, a survivor, a mother, and whether you know it or not, you're the love of Maverick's life."

I stare at her. She's serious. "I'm not."

"Trust me, I'm right on this. Look, you'll be his ol' lady soon enough, and I don't wanna step on your toes because you're good for him. You're good for this place. So, I'm asking you if I can stick around. I'm not here to win Maverick over, I have no interest in him anymore. I have a kid, and he'd love Ella."

"What do you do with your kid when you're off . . . killing people?"

She laughs. "I have a great friend."

"I've never met a killer before," I mutter.

She stares out across the field, "Sure you have, Rylee. You just didn't know it."

My mind goes back to Mav and the fact he's killed Grant. The sickness returns, and I flop back, throwing my hand over my eyes. "How do you do it? Act like this is all normal?"

"I don't think about it. I make jokes. I laugh a lot. I do whatever it takes to keep going. Whatever Mav does, it's all to protect you and Ella. Don't be so hard on the guy. He loves you."

"I needed control of the situation, and he promised me I could have it, but then took it back last minute."

"Boo-fucking-hoo," she mutters, and I uncover my eyes to look at her. "Your ex was a piece of shit. We all know it. I mean, that's what you're talking about right, the fact Mav took him out? I did my research and yah know what I found? He once attended a call out to a woman in distress. She was drunk and your man raped her. She had a hazy memory of it a few days after it happened, made a complaint, but it didn't go further because she was too drunk! Imagine that, how she must have felt to know her word wasn't good enough over the cops. He was a bastard and he deserved whatever Mav did."

"It's not about what he did. It's that he took the decision away from me."

"Because you made the wrong one," Rosey says, pushing to stand. "He would have gone on to torture and abuse some other poor fucker and that would have been on you. Mav simply followed your wishes, but with a little twist." She heads for the clubhouse. "If you ask me, he did the world a favour."

I hear Brea wailing from inside Mav's office and a tear rolls down my cheek. She doesn't deserve this pain. Whatever Crow did, he was her son and she loved him. Hadley squeezes my hand. "It's been a crazy day."

"Poor Brea," I mutter.

"It's going to be hard for her, for all of us." A tear slips down her cheek, and I pull her into a hug. Just because Mav and Crow didn't get along, doesn't mean his sisters were the same. They loved their stepbrother. "Meli and Rosey were the best of friends growing up and now she's killed our brother."

"Sounds like there was a lot that went on before. What Crow did to her was so wrong," I begin.

Hadley sniffles, wiping her eyes on her sleeves. "I know. I don't want to make excuses, but my dad played a huge part in how Crow behaved. I just can't believe he's gone."

The office door opens, and Maverick glares at us for a second before shouting for Hadley to join them in the office.

CHAPTER TWENTY

MAVERICK

Hadley steps inside, and I close the door. I need to speak to Rylee desperately, but there's so much shit to sort through. Meli admitted what had happened to her the second Mum and I confronted her. Now, they're all crying, and I have no idea what the fuck to do next. "We can't change what's happened," I begin after filling Hadley in on everything and their sniffles die down. "We have to make the changes so we don't slip back to those places again. Dad took his eye off the ball and nothing was good from that point on. We can't sit here and pretend he was a saint because he wasn't, and Meli has proved that. What kind of father says shit like that?" I fume. "She was a kid!"

"I'll never forgive myself," sobs Mum, and Meli grips her hand tightly.

"It wasn't your fault."

"I was so busy trying to repair the damage I did and I didn't notice. It was totally my fault. I'm supposed to protect you."

Meli wraps her arms around Mum and whispers into her ear, gently rocking her back and forth. "We'll heal from this," I say. "That will be our biggest 'fuck you' to Dad."

"Is Rosey sticking around?" asks Meli.

I shrug. "I need to talk to her next."

"I understand why she did what she did. I love Crow, but what he did was wrong," says Meli. "He never stood a chance with Dad treating him how he did."

"Agreed," I mutter. "But I've just found Rylee and I don't want Rosey to fuck that up. There's one other thing," I say, and they all look at me. "Rosey has a kid and it's Dad's."

○○

I call Rosey next, leaving Mum and the twins to comfort one another. They'll pull together and get each other through this mess.

Rosey drops in the seat opposite my desk and props her feet up on the shiny oak. "What a fucking day," she huffs, looking around the office. "You did alright for yourself."

"Why didn't you come to me?" I mutter.

"Before I killed half your family?" she asks. "Or after your dad and brother fucked my life up?"

"Both. When you decided to go, I thought it was best for you. I thought you'd get a fucking nice job and marry a good man."

"My job is cool," she says, grinning. "I mean, the working hours aren't great and they're not very child-friendly, but I get by."

"Your job is insane. Rosey, what the fuck happened?"

"It's what I do and I enjoy it. Besides, fate brought us back together." She smirks. "That, and the fact I needed to kill your dad. I can help you."

I sigh heavily. It's been a long day. "With?"

"Men like Grant Carter. Nice move, by the way. I'm gonna try the boat thing sometime."

"I don't need help."

"Mav, I can off these men like Medusa turned men to stone. You wanna help rescue battered women, and I want to give them justice."

"Carter was different. We don't plan on killing every arsehole."

"Different because you love his wife."

"They weren't married. And yes, because I fucking love Rylee and Ella with all my heart, and I'll do anything to protect them."

Rosey smiles. "I'm so glad you've found her. She's good for you. I like her. Look, Mav, I'm offering to help. Please let me. I can be good for this place."

"You wanna move back here?" She nods, and I laugh. "With my dad's kid?" She nods again.

"He's a great kid. Kind and funny. You'll like him."

"I don't know if I have the strength to deal with you right now," I mutter, scrubbing my hands over my tired face.

"Sure you do, Mav. We'll be a great team." She heads for the door.

"We're not a team, Rosey. I'm the President, and you're . . . I don't even know."

"Pulling rank on me already, I love that," she says, grinning.

∞

It's almost seven in the evening when I'm done talking with just about every fucker in this damn club. Everyone except Rylee. Hadley is on the couch, but Rylee is no longer beside her. "She's gone to bed," she says before I've asked. "Guess she got tired of waiting around."

I find her lying on her bed with her back to me, but I can tell by the rise and fall of her body that she's still awake. I shrug out of my kutte and kick off my boots. "I am so sorry," I whisper as I climb onto the bed behind her. I gently run my fingers up her arm. "I didn't mean to put everyone else before you. It just turned out that way and every fucker had something to say in church so—"

"It's fine."

"It's not fine, Rylee. Stop letting me off the hook," I mutter, sighing.

"What do you want me to do?"

"I dunno, shout, yell, cry?"

"I'm all outta tears, Mav. I got nothing left."

I nuzzle into her neck, breathing in her flowery scent. "Everything feels so messed up."

She turns over, propping her head up with a pillow. "I wanted to tell you about Meli. It was just so huge—" I press a finger to her lips and kiss her nose.

"It wasn't your fault. I get why you didn't tell me."

"I feel like since I came, trouble's just followed me. I should have listened to you about Crow. He tried to take me away from here," she says, her eyes watering.

"Rosey told me. I shouldn't have left you alone. I thought you'd be safe in my club and I was fucking wrong. I've been wrong about so much."

RYLEE

Maverick looks so tired and broken. I've never seen the defeated look in his eye that sits there right now. He's done enough apologising and explaining for one day, so I wrap my arms around his neck and gently pull him to lie against my chest. I run my fingers up and down his back and occasionally drop a chaste kiss on his head. Within minutes, he's asleep.

We stay like that for a few hours before we're woken by Ella's screams. We both dive up in a panic. "It's okay," I whisper. "It's just Ella having a bad dream. She does it sometimes."

Mav lets out a slow breath. "I'll go. You sleep."

I smile as he disappears into Ella's room. I love that he cares about her. When he still hasn't returned twenty minutes later, I pop my head around her door and suck in a surprised breath. Mav is sleeping with his head propped against her headboard, and Ella is lying across him with her head resting against his chest, his arms wrapped tightly around her tiny body. It's the cutest thing I've ever seen, and I spend a good ten minutes watching them sleep.

Morning arrives and Mav returns, stretching out his arms as he groans. "Comfy night?" I ask, grinning.

"She needs a bigger bed," he grumbles.

"It was sweet of you to comfort her like that," I say quietly.

"I'll always be there for Ella, Rylee. She's a part of you."

At breakfast, it's the usual chaos, and for a few minutes, it's almost like yesterday didn't happen. I never realised how much Crow's mood hung over everyone, but I don't miss his scowling face today. I think everyone feels the same, except Brea of course, who remains quiet as she sips her coffee.

"Is it just me, or does the tension seem to have gone?" whispers Mav, and I nod in agreement. "Even Meli is smiling," he adds. She's laughing with Grim and Hadley and it's a beautiful sight to see. Ripper isn't hanging over her anymore.

Rosey joins us. She's in her pyjamas and her hair is a bird's nest. "Morning, roomies," she says, grinning and taking a seat beside me. Brea scowls and leaves the kitchen. Rosey lowers her eyes for a second before plastering a fake smile on her face and reaching for the eggs. "I slept like a baby."

"Wiping out a few men can tire a person out," says Grim, and Rosey winks at him.

"We have to move on from that," she says. "It's done."

"You might want to look less gloating about the fact my brother is now dead," mutters Hadley.

"Yeah, Rosey, tone it down a little," adds Mav. "Emotions are raw, especially for my mum. You wanna stay here, then sort it out."

She lowers her eyes again, and I can't help but think she's nervous. Despite the bravado she came with, she feels vulnerable here with all the guys who know the real her. "So, how long do you plan on staying?" I ask to change the subject.

"I'm not sure," she says, glancing at Maverick, "If everyone is happy for me to stay for a while, I'll go and collect Ollie today. I'd like him to meet you all."

"Fantastic. I can't wait to meet him," I say, a little too jovial. Hadley and Meli remain silent, and the laughter from moments ago has now long gone.

I begin to clear the table just to avoid the frosty atmosphere. Mav comes up behind me and places his hands on my hips. "We need to talk, baby," he whispers in my ear.

"I'll gladly leave this room," I whisper back, and he takes me to his office.

"Things got a little frosty in there," he says, and I nod.

"I think Rosey isn't as happy and badass as she makes out. She's finding it hard to be like that here because you all know her. She's working out who to be right now, the badass killer or the vulnerable little girl you all knew."

Maverick grins, leaning back in his chair. "Look at you taking your role seriously."

"Role?" I repeat.

"As my ol' lady." He stares, waiting for my reaction, but I don't flinch. Being at this man's side, I'd be mad not to want it. "You seem okay with that."

"Why wouldn't I be?"

"You serious? You'll be my ol' lady?" I nod, and he jumps from his chair, rushing to me and wrapping me in his arms. "I didn't think you were ready, but it just slipped out." He kisses me like I'm his lifeline before releasing me and staring at me like he can't quite believe I've agreed to this. "I thought you'd still be mad about Grant and everything," he admits.

"Oh, I'm still mad, Mav," I say, and his smile fades. "I'm mad as hell that you went behind my back, disrespected my wishes, and lied about where you were. If I'm gonna be your ol' lady, you need to start listening to me," I say before adding a playful smile. "But I also know you did all that for me and Ella. You wanted to free us, and how can I be mad when you're the one who saved us in the first place? Without you, who knows where I'd be. Maybe I'd be the one at the bottom of the sea. Truth is, I love you. And yeah, we might disagree on how you handle certain situations, but that's normal, right?"

"He was never gonna leave you alone. But I was listening when you said you had unanswered questions. He didn't register Ella at birth because he was worried you'd eventually find some way to get her a passport and you'd leave. He was always plotting ways to keep you caged and he would have found a way to get you back in that prison if we'd have let him ride off into the sunset."

"What will happen to his new girlfriend and kid?"

"She'll be fine. He gave her the whole 'it's not you, it's me' speech right before he was about to leave. Ghost overheard him on the phone at the docks. He threw his mobile in the water right after. So apart from a broken heart, she'll survive, and we potentially saved her from a life like you had. No one will miss him, Rylee. Ella will eventually forget too. We just have to keep giving her good memories to replace the bad."

"We're so lucky to have found you," I mutter.

"No, Rylee, I'm the lucky one. When I came back here, I felt so out of my depth, but having you by my side makes me see so clearly. We're gonna help so many victims and give them a better life. We can open some new businesses and give vulnerable people a job. We're gonna turn this club around, and that's all because of you. Together, we're gonna be amazing."

I move to his desk, sitting before him and wrapping my arms around his neck. "I love you so much."

"I love you too, Bandia."

"Goddess, right?" I say, and he grins, nodding.

"My Bandia, my Queen, my life."

THE END

A note from me to you

The Perished Riders series is my second MC series. If you haven't read the first, go check it out on Amazon.

For more books in this series, you'll find them here: https://linktr.ee/NicolaJaneUK

If you enjoyed this story, please leave a review or rating on Amazon or Goodreads. It helps independent authors like myself, an enormous amount.

I'm a UK author, based in Nottinghamshire. I live with my husband of many years, our two teenage boys and our four little dogs. I write MC and Mafia romance with plenty of drama and chaos. I also love to read similar books. My favourite author is Tillie Cole. Before I became a full-time author, I was a teaching assistant working in a primary school.

If you'd like to follow my writing journey, join my readers group on Facebook, the link is above. You can also use that link if you're a book blogger, I'd love you to sign up to my team.

Printed in Great Britain
by Amazon